Sankar and the Chemistry Crime Committee

Sankar and the Chemistry Crime Committee

by

G. K. Vemulapalli

ISBN: **978-0-615-26467-7**

Library of Congress Control Number: **2008908346**

For

Carolyn, Sarita and Ravi

Contents

Chapter 1

Age of Accountability

This is the first case of suicide during my tenure as the head of the department," Professor Czerny commented.

I am sure he didn't mean it that way, but it sounded as though there was a quota for the number of suicides during his administration.

"Yes. I'm quite upset about the whole thing," he continued. "If it is in my power, I'll see that it never happens again."

This was my first meeting with the professor and I had no idea what he was talking about. Who committed suicide? And when? Why did Professor Czerny think I should be informed about this?

He must have noticed my puzzled expression, for he said, "I am assuming you heard about the tragedy over the weekend?"

"No, Dr. Czerny."

I reminded him that I had joined the chemistry department just a month back, as the university was slowing down for the Christmas-New Year break.

"Nevertheless, you must be a very dedicated researcher to be unaware of what everyone on campus has been talking about."

Professor Czerny proceeded to explain. About ten o'clock Saturday evening a graduate student, Gregg Westover, was found dead at his desk by a campus policewoman going around the building checking for unlocked doors.

"They tell me that he drank soda laced with cyanide, probably sometime late in the afternoon."

"Late afternoon, Saturday! The building is usually deserted." Even more than usual, I thought, since it was the weekend before spring semester classes started.

I had met Gregg Westover. He and I were in the same research group - the one supervised by Professor Franklin Turner. However, we had nothing in common by way of scientific activities and our labs were, as it happened, at opposite corners of the fourth floor. The short time I had spent in the department had not given me a chance to get well acquainted with any of the faculty or the grad students.

*   *   *

Earlier in the day, I was behind a gurgling vacuum pump, pouring sizzling liquid nitrogen into a cold trap, when I heard the knock.

"Come in," I yelled at the top of my voice which probably couldn't be heard over the din of the machine.

No one came in. I couldn't drop what I was doing and run to the door. I wouldn't dare to hurry in such a congested lab, a room of a hundred and twenty square feet packed with equipment, books and chemicals. First I'd have to go around the big rack full of intricately connected glass tubing that could go bang and break at the slightest provocation. Then I'd have to weave my way between the other side of the rack and a lab bench adorned with chemicals and distillation apparatus. Beyond that I'd have to avoid a collision with a filing cabinet and a book shelf, overloaded with copies of the *Journal of the American Chemical Society*. By the time I might have managed to get to the door, the person on the other side could have gone clear across campus.

Accepted custom does not require knocking on the door before entering a laboratory. If you want to talk to someone working in a lab, you just open the door and walk in. Then you wait, without saying anything, until the person is ready to put down his or her work and pay attention to you. You should, of course, keep your hands in your pockets to avoid touching things in a moment of absentmindedness. Even first year students know this. Only insurance salesmen and new secretaries seem to have difficulty grasping the concept.

On that day, which happened to be the first day of the spring semester, I was preparing to do what I thought would be a decisive experiment. Not decisive enough to change the course of science or, for that matter, even to make any significant impact in my own obscure area of research, but decisive enough to get me a publication in spite of the reviewers' usual nit-picking and nasty comments and editors' unwillingness to be impartial.

I had had about twenty minutes of uninterrupted activity when I heard the knock again. I was then checking the electrical connections to a dysfunctional vacuum gauge with an obdurate needle. I didn't want to put up with the irritation of listening to someone knocking on the door for the rest of the day, so I hurried to the door after extricating myself from the sinuous wires.

Swinging the door open, I faced a fair-skinned, blonde goddess who happened to be Professor Czerny's secretary with the Latina name of Cathy Quintaro. "Dr. Czerny wants to see you. It's urgent. He's waiting."

I made sure there was enough liquid nitrogen in the cold traps to last during my conference with the head before joining Cathy in the corridor.

"Any idea why Professor Czerny wants to see me?" I asked as I kept pace with Cathy's energetic gait.

"No."

Even before she said that, I had fabricated a theory which, unfortunately, turned out to be wrong.

I was then a post-doctoral associate – post-doc for short – meaning that I had earned my doctorate but was stuck in limbo between that stage and getting a job with some level of security. Consequently, I went from university to university, to wherever the grant money was available at the moment, and did research in some professor's laboratory. I didn't have the status of the faculty, who are largely free to do what they choose, or that of the staff personnel, who cannot be fired without a just cause, or that of the students who, in a modern university, can and do claim the privileges of consumers. For me the length of an appointment at any university depended on research funds being available and on pleasing a few people - mainly the faculty who direct the research - and no less on not antagonizing the rest of the academic community.

For years I had been looking - desperately looking - for a job that would give me some continuity. I was getting tired of being a transient scientist going from one campus to the next, following the tides of grant money. I didn't mind the frequent moves, even though my wife, Meera, complained bitterly before, during and after each move. I enjoyed living in different parts of the country. The price I had to pay for it, unfortunately, was high, too high. Each time we moved, I had to give up a research project before it could be extended to reap the full benefits. Living thus as a scientific migrant worker, I had not been able to build a CV that would make anyone take a second look.

The brutal reality was that if I didn't get a faculty position soon, I'd have as much chance of getting one in future as a poor, forty-year old Victorian spinster had of finding a husband. The universities preferred young, aggressive candidates, fresh out of graduate school or mature, established fund-raisers. I was neither.

Now Professor Czerny happened to be the head of the department, the head honcho, as my boss, Professor Turner, would say. A Mercedes brought Professor Czerny to work and was parked on a spot reserved for him twenty-four hours a day. I was told that the head of the department made two and half times the average faculty salary – more than five times mine. I had been hoping to meet him ever since I arrived in Gadsden four weeks earlier. Since my intent was to tout my accomplishments - I had applied for an advertised faculty position in the department, even before coming to Gadsden - I was waiting for the right moment to meet Professor Czerny. I knew that all my papers were in order and the necessary recommendation letters had been sent on time. A generic letter from the head informed me of that fact, but I didn't know whether the selection process had yet begun. During the past ten years I had failed in every attempt to secure a faculty post in a research university, so you can see why I was anxious and apprehensive.

The first thought that came to my mind, when Cathy mentioned Professor Czerny's wish to see me, was that the department might need someone to take over a course or two. Here I was, just starting as a research associate, ready to take up teaching duties at a moment's notice. It would be a giant step for me toward a permanent academic position and, at the same time, it would save the department some agony since they wouldn't have to search far and wide to get someone at such short notice.

But even as I was dreaming of my future in academia, with a greater salary and far better security, another thought in the back of my mind warned me not to get my hopes up too high. The department had more than thirty faculty members. About twenty-five of them were research-active professors, each of them with five to fifteen coworkers: graduate students struggling for their doctorates and post-docs, like me, honored with degrees but not with secure jobs. Given those numbers, it was unlikely that the head of the department would be looking desperately for someone, at this late hour, to fill a vacancy.

"It's going to be an interview for a job," I told myself to banish my doubts.

As Cathy opened the door, Professor Czerny got up and extended his hand across the mammoth desk.

"Come in. Come in, Sankar. We haven't been formally introduced but I'm sure we know of each other." I guessed that he was in his mid fifties. Broad shouldered and slightly overweight, Dr. Czerny gave the impression of a man who was once trim and athletic. He was very nearly bald and wore glasses that seemed to hang on his face without a frame. Dr. Czerny looked straight into my eyes as he shook my hand vigorously.

The office was spacious - very spacious by academic standards - and seemed to contain equal numbers of plants and books. Professor Czerny's jacket was neatly hung on a rack in the corner and a clip-on tie - perhaps to be worn on more formal occasions - was within arm's reach. The cap of a Mont Blanc pen, protruding out of the pocket of his expensive shirt, did not escape my attention. I started to feel uncomfortable, as I usually do in the presence of authority.

"Glad you could come," he said.

I remembered to give a firm American handshake. From the warmth in his greeting and the fact that he already knew my abbreviated name, which is the only one I use, I thought we would be discussing a faculty appointment for me.

I was thoroughly mistaken.

*   *   *

"I want to ask for a little bit of assistance on matters concerning Gregg's suicide. If you can't spare the time, say so. You are under no obligation."

I was thoroughly baffled. What type of assistance? Why should this concern me in the first place?

"What can I do?" My voice must have sounded plaintive.

"I've appointed a committee of three faculty members to look into this matter. I'd like to have a broader base for the committee. That is to say I'd like to hear from non-faculty personnel as well. Would you be able to spare a few hours of your time for the committee work?"

That didn't clear my bafflement. A graduate student swallows cyanide and the head of the department appoints a committee! For what? I had been told that Gadsden City had a high crime rate. Were the police so busy that they couldn't find time to investigate a suicide?

"I thought the police usually take care of these matters."

"Yes, they do, Sankar. Indeed I've already spent several hours talking to the homicide guys. But there are issues that go beyond the police investigation."

That explained nothing. The original puzzle remained a puzzle.

"What can a committee do?" I said.

"A lot, Sankar. I see the work of the committee as complementing that of the police."

My face must have betrayed a total lack of understanding, for Professor Czerny went on with his explanation.

"You see, Sankar, we are in the age of accountability. Yes, that's what I think it should be called. For every incident, however insignificant it might be, we are asked to answer a whole barrage of questions. Think of the case in front of you. I mean Gregg's suicide. There will be questions about chemical stores procedures. Was the cyanide too readily accessible? What precautions should be taken in storing dangerous chemicals? There will be questions about the atmosphere in the department. Are we - as a department - putting too much pressure on our graduate students? Do we need counseling services for the departmental personnel? Did the research director - I'm sure it's Professor Turner, I have such a hard time keeping up with who works with whom - show sufficient empathy for the student? Could he - the research director - have prevented this suicide with some tea and sympathy? I have said more than once that a research director must not act like a boss in an industrial lab. He must behave like a member of the family - the more experienced member. Remember, Sankar, that a university is supposed to be the *Alma Mater*. Those words remind us of our true responsibility as faculty members ... and as post-doc's who will one day be involved in training students. I can go on and on, but I won't. What I need are well-thought answers for the type of questions the people out there are going to ask. We have to be prepared, Sankar. We can't wait until the questions start pouring in."

I must say that I was impressed by Professor Czerny's eloquence even though I was still vague about what the committee and I, as a member of the committee, would be doing.

"Is there any particular reason you want me on the committee?"

"Well, I want input from outside the faculty ranks. And I don't want a graduate student poking his nose into sensitive issues. You are relatively new to the department and might see things with a totally different perspective."

My mind was stuck on the word 'input.' I never liked that word being used except in computerese.

"Will you serve on the committee?"

"Yes, of course, Professor Czerny."

A rational answer would have been to say no. My liberation from post-doctoral under-employment depended entirely on publishing a steady stream of articles. That meant I should have chained myself to the apparatus - my vacuum rack - and ignored the rest of the world. I had once thought of sending Meera and our nine-year old son, Jay, back to India for an extended period so that I could devote uninterrupted sixteen-hour days to lab work until I had a permanent position. I was glad, however, that I hadn't suggested the idea to Meera. For when experiments went wrong, as they often did, I depended on the solace of their company for continuing on the research projects. Without their sympathy I might have thrown in the towel long ago.

Why did I agree to be on the committee? Was I swayed by Professor Czerny's eloquence? More likely it was my propensity to be intimidated by professors that made me say yes.

I still didn't have the slightest idea what I would be doing as a member of the committee. Committee for what? To prevent suicides? To investigate crime? What was really worrying Professor Czerny about this case? I didn't know how to put these questions to Professor Czerny without trying his patience. I had just had my first chance to meet him and participate in a conversation. This could be valuable for my professional advancement. I didn't want to antagonize Professor Czerny by sounding arrogant with constant questioning or by appearing stupid.

Professor Czerny had been talking in a leisurely manner, but I knew, all along, that there was an invisible clock silently ticking and when it chimed - so to speak - I would be shown the door. The chiming, it turned out, was done by Cathy Quintaro, who opened the door without knocking. "I just wanted to remind you of the luncheon appointment with the Provost."

"True... Thanks for telling me, Cathy. We're almost finished here... You have any questions, Sankar?"

"None at this time."

"Good. Professor Fuller will chair the committee. You will hear from him soon. And here's a note Cathy prepared. Says a few words about the committee."

I wanted to ask Professor Czerny about my application for the faculty position. Had they started looking at the files? What chances did I have? But I didn't know how to insert it gracefully into the conversation. So I got up quietly and walked toward the door while silently blaming myself for not having the courage to ask Professor Czerny about what concerned me most.

"Sankar," called Professor Czerny as I was opening the door.

"Yes, Professor Czerny?" I turned around to find the head of the department standing and looking very solemn.

"Since I became the head of this department, thanks to the efforts of many individuals, we have made tremendous progress. Our department is now rated in the top third of the PhD granting chemistry departments. There is no reason why we can't be in the top five per cent, if we work hard and pull together. We have the best climate and far, far better living conditions than anywhere else in the country. Ours is a growing state and we have an administration committed to nothing less than the very best. I'd say to any talented scientist, this is where the real action is going to be - not in Boston, not in the Bay area. And I'm going to see that we live up to our full potential. If there are any problems in the department, however small they are, I want to be the first to know. I want to fix them - as much as I can - before they become unmanageable."

It was really an impressive pep talk. I suppose I'd have clapped, if I were in a crowd. But being alone, I mumbled a weak "I'll-do-my-best." Then I was overcome by a sudden surge of courage, enough to remind Professor Czerny about the vacancy in the department.

"What faculty position?" He asked to my surprise.

"The one advertised last semester. You sent me a letter acknowledging my application."

"Linda must've sent the standard letter. Well, I haven't yet appointed a committee to screen the applicants. That's because the dean is hesitating. He's a timid man, at least by my standards. He doesn't want us to interview the candidates until all the kinks in the budget are worked out. If we do have an opening in the department, we will give very serious consideration to your application. And what you do on this committee will certainly give you an edge on the other applicants."

Not a reassuring answer in spite of those encouraging last words, I thought as I slunk out of the office.

*   *   *

I read the sheet Professor Czerny handed me as I left the office. The committee was dubbed Ad Hoc Committee for Personnel Affairs. The chairman of the committee was identified as Professor James Fuller. The other members were Professors Niles Baxter and Richard Blackwell. My own name did not appear on the sheet, presumably because I hadn't yet been consulted when it was typed. There was a page of text describing the committee's mandate. I browsed through it quickly.

".... keeping in mind the modern trend toward accountability on all levels of academic activity, the committee is urged to spare no efforts in its investigation of all aspects of this truly unfortunate incident."

Chapter 2

Professor Turner Gives
his Okay

I 'd been uneasy in the presence of Professor Czerny, but the moment I left his office my uneasiness turned into misery; for I realized then that I had violated one of the most important protocols of academic life. I should have consulted Professor Turner, my supervisor, before saying yea or nay to Professor Czerny.

I was called - in official documents - a research associate. My appointment papers were signed by the president of the University of Gadsden after they hopped from desk to desk and eventually reached his. But the president's signature was a mere formality. The money for my appointment came from a grant Professor Turner had received from a government agency. It was his money, as they say in academic circles, except for the overhead skimmed right off the top by the university administration. Within the broad guidelines set forth by the granting agency, Professor Turner could do whatever he wanted with that money. He could have hired graduate students, technical specialists, undergraduate students or even secretaries instead of me. He could have bought more equipment instead of hiring anyone. Thus it was he who had the real power over me. He could tell me, at any moment, to pack my belongings and leave, and the strength and scholarship of the university would come swiftly to his side.

Whether you are paid on a research grant or not, it's generally accepted that your professor has what may be called the intellectual property rights over you. To have anything to do with Professor X, when you are under the supervision of Professor Y, is asking for trouble - sometimes very serious.

I had a lesson on this aspect of academic life during my first post-doctoral appointment. One of the grad students of a professor - I'll call him Professor X - came to talk to me about an article he couldn't understand. We talked on and off for a few weeks about the stuff in that article. Well, one thing led to another and we were able to extend one of the ideas in that article into a slightly different area. Exhilarated at our accomplishment, we wrote a short note and, to our pleasant surprise, it was accepted promptly for publication in a not totally obscure journal.

The whole thing could have ended happily had not the grad student called everyone's attention to our modest achievement. He bragged to other grad students that he and I were able to get a paper out in record time. When Professor X heard about this, he became raging mad. I was accused of stealing one of his brand new ideas. I was blamed for distracting a grad student from the proper course of studies. I protested saying that what we did was kilometers away from the professor's area of research and that I did not, at any time, entice the student to work with me. My protests didn't do any good and Professor X continued on his war path. Some weeks later I had to face the head of the department who told me that I should have consulted Professor X before doing anything with his grad student and that, even if I were the true discoverer of the idea, I should not have published it behind the professor's back. What I did, working as I did with a grad student without his supervisor's knowledge, showed a lack of collegial spirit. I often wondered whether this incident had anything to do with the fact that my job at that learned institution was terminated a few months later.

As it turned out I got away unharmed, relatively speaking. The grad student had it worse. He had to leave the university a semester later without a degree. The last time I heard about him, he was in the wilderness of Wyoming selling insurance or shoes. I never thought that a small article on an unimportant idea in a rarely read specialized journal would cause so much damage to one of the authors.

*   *   *

As I thought about this little bit of history, I was aware that my worries at the moment were exaggerated. Professor X was a real basket case whose academic success depended equally on his ability to corral hard working students and on his incurable paranoia. Professor Turner, with whom I had had only good relations so far, was a more easy going man. If he were indeed irritated, he would say so and forgive and forget it next day. Yet I wasn't ready to face Professor Turner until I had carefully worked out a strategy to inform him about my membership on the committee. It was, after all, a serious mistake on my part to take up any activities that would curtail my research productivity without consulting the boss first.

I was hungry. But the peanut butter sandwich, prepared by my loving wife Meera and now resting on the book shelf above, did not appeal to me. Peanut butter sandwiches have a special property. They may be eaten a day or two after they are made without loss of taste or texture. Thus I rationalized as I ambled to the cafeteria to order myself a cheese enchilada, salad and coffee. I had another good reason for going to the cafeteria. I wanted to get hold of the morning newspaper and read what was said about Gregg's suicide. There were several discarded newspapers next to the dirty dish rack. I collected what I wanted and moved to the least crowded part of the cafeteria.

The Gadsden Gazette printed the news about Gregg's suicide at the end of the Metro Section. No details were given even though Professor Czerny was quoted extensively. It was a loss to the department, he had said. The faculty took pride in cultivating a personal relation with each of the graduate students, even though there were more than a hundred in the department. Each student was given individual attention and was never treated as a part of the mob, unlike in East coast or California universities. Professor Czerny wished that Gregg Westover had been able to visit him and bring his concerns to the attention of the administration. A very serious tragedy could have been prevented.

I didn't blame Professor Czerny for having said what he was expected to say. However, there wasn't any useful information in the article.

Gadsden Grizzly, the student newspaper, paid more attention to the story. "Stress Leads to Suicide," the title of the article proclaimed.

Gregg Westover's dead body, sprawled on the laboratory floor - his face next to a pool of vomit - was found by Linda Bracamonte, a campus security officer, on Saturday around 9 P.M. as she was making sure that all the rooms in the building were properly locked. She checked the pulse and immediately called Capt. Noonan, head of Campus Security who promptly called the homicide detectives of the city police department. He also called Professor Czerny. Professor Czerny was quick to suggest to Capt. Noonan that they should look into the possibility of cyanide poisoning, which could render the victim unconscious within two minutes of ingestion, killing him before he could realize what was happening. Professor Czerny's idea turned out to be right: it was a case of cyanide poisoning, though the police couldn't find a cyanide bottle on Gregg's desk or in the lab where his desk was located. Suicide seemed the likely cause of death even though the officers investigating the case had not ruled out other possibilities.

The article was followed by another in which the president of the Graduate Student Association, Lynn Richter, was interviewed. The graduate students at the University of Gadsden were overworked and underpaid. They spent more hours grading papers, conducting labs and tutoring than graduate students at comparable institutions. Gadsden grad students were paid fifteen per cent less than the national average. Because of the excessive demands on their time, graduate students at the University of Gadsden had fewer opportunities for advancement and professional success. No wonder that there had been a great deal of despair. One only hoped that Gregg's suicide was an isolated case and not an indication of a trend.

I could not help wondering about Lynn Richter, how she looked and what she did. In my imagination, she was a graduate student in one of those social sciences, like social psychology. Recently divorced. Getting by on a minuscule spousal maintenance and stingy quarter time salary from the university. I put her age at thirty-five and made her a mother of two rowdy boys in grade school. Totally dissatisfied with the educational system and..... I put breaks on my mental peregrination at that point and wondered why I had stepped into the world of fantasy. It is true: theories abound when facts are few.

I had to get back to facts. But first I had to get Professor Turner's approval.

*   *   *

The cheese enchilada lunch gave me sufficient courage to face Professor Turner. As I entered his office through the open door, I noticed that he was poring over a contour map, spread on top of the books and papers on his disorderly desk. The walls of the crowded office were covered with relief maps of the southwestern states.

"Beth and I were here over the weekend," he said pointing to a spot on the map. "You take the Anasazi trail. When you go past Corrales Peak you get off the trail and bushwhack your way down for a couple of miles. It's a gorgeous spot with an inviting pool and a bunch of lush cottonwoods. You should go there one of these days. Jay would have a hell of a good time."

He need not have given me that piece of information; I'd have guessed his weekend activities from the odor of campfires emanating from the cap he dumped on the computer keyboard. Nevertheless I was glad to hear that. Talk about outdoors cheered my boss. Maybe I could gently break the news in this harmonious atmosphere.

"When did you come back?"

"Last night. We had to cover the last mile of the trail in the dark. Beth was furious and bitched all the way."

"Did you hear about Gregg Westover?"

"Yes. Czerny left a message on the answering machine at home. I didn't check my calls until this morning though. I also had an e-mail from him this morning."

"I also heard about it just today."

"You should see our e-mail correspondence," Professor Turner said ignoring my words. Then he turned around, clicked the mouse a few times, snatched the papers out of the printer's mouth and gave them to me.

"Read it."

I did what I was told to do.

Frank:

I've been calling you throughout the weekend. I regret to tell you that your graduate student, Gregg W., committed suicide on Saturday. I want to assure you that the department is ready to help you & your group in dealing with this tragic situation.

I must tell you that I feel your leaving town just before classes start is quite inappropriate. After all, this is when the students come up with lots of questions on requirements, registration, syllabus etc. This is also when students are in need of tea and sympathy. A faculty member must have compelling reasons to be unavailable at this time. I cannot help thinking that if you had been in town Gregg might have called you to talk about his troubles instead of grabbing a cyanide bottle.

I want to assure you that I am writing this letter as a concerned friend and not as the head of the department.

David

Professor Turner's reply followed.

David:

You might not know, shielded as you are with all the administrative paper work, that Gregg has been in my group for only two and half months. For more than a year before that he was in Blackwell's group. I have no idea what problems he had then to make him switch directors. During the time he was in my group he came to see me twice. I did not go after him with a daily list of things to do. I let my students progress at their own pace. I DO NOT micro-manage their lives as many in the faculty do these days.

I am sure Gregg could have found sympathetic ears outside the chemistry building had he tried. Besides, no one goes to the boss for sympathy.

I believe your concern about my being out of town is unwarranted. Any student coming for advice at the last moment should be discouraged. If we can't teach them to plan ahead nothing else we teach matters. I know we are supposed to treat students as consumers/clients. (DAMN THE WORDS!) I just don't subscribe to that philosophy. We only cripple the students by demanding nothing of them, and they could never go beyond depending on us.

I want to assure you that I am writing this as a friend and not as a critic of the administration.

Frank

"What do you think?" The question came even before I finished reading the epistles.

I knew enough not to answer. It turned out, fortunately, that Professor Turner was not expecting a reply. He went on to the next topic.

"I come to the department this morning and what do I find? The graduate course I was supposed to do was canceled. On the first day of classes without the slightest hint! All that time I spent preparing for it was wasted, completely wasted."

"I am sorry to hear that."

"Some idiot dean evidently decided at the last minute to drop graduate courses with fewer than seven students. So I am assigned to teach freshman chemistry for cowboys. On a junior high level of course. I'm really pissed off at the stupid administration. Anyway, I've been looking at a picture book of chemistry, supposedly the textbook for this course. That's what the damned textbooks are these days - pictures and no text."

I assumed that was his explanation for not taking any more interest in the untimely death of one of his graduate students.

"Dr. Czerny called me to his office to tell me about Gregg," I wanted to introduce the topic gently.

"So you had an audience with the great Poo Bah himself!"

I once knew a fellow who could only speak in scientific jargon. He used to say that an attractive force could develop between a pair of professors only when hell was about to reach absolute zero temperature. From the snide remarks Professor Turner had been making since I joined his lab, from the e-mail I had just read, it was clear that there was no love lost between him and Professor Czerny.

"Professor Czerny had an interesting idea." I said. It was time to mention the committee.

"What's that?"

"There could be some nagging questions when somebody kills himself in the laboratory. He thought a committee should look into all possible ramifications."

I was surprised to find that I could state the committee's mission so well. I hadn't been sure that I understood it myself before that moment. I was equally surprised at Professor Turner's reaction.

"A committee?"

"Yes."

"So we have a Chemistry Crime Committee. Is that it?"

"No. It's called Ad Hoc Committee for..."

"The name doesn't matter, but I expected something like that."

"Did you know about the committee?"

"No, but I expected Czerny would do that."

The reasoning wasn't obvious to me. At any rate I was relieved that I didn't have to defend the need for the committee.

"You know why? Don't you?" Professor Turner continued.

I said, "No."

"Whenever the slime ball smells opportunity, however small it might be, he appoints a committee."

"What opportunity?" It was a simple case of suicide. So I was told. I didn't see how anyone could find opportunity for anything there.

"What opportunity? You don't see one and I don't see one. That's because we both think like normal human beings. But Czerny is different."

It made no sense to me. I tried to follow Professor Turner's reasoning.

"He thinks differently. He twists everything to his advantage. A couple of years ago there were complaints by a few students about a course. It turned out that all they wanted was some assurance that the instructor would promptly post the answers for the homework. The students went to see Czerny first, instead of talking to the instructor. And before we knew it, we had a committee and a big document on how to provide quality instruction. Czerny pedaled that document all the way up the administration tower, from floor to floor, and got a healthy chunk of money for teaching improvement. Of course, once he got the money he spent it on his own research - every cent of it."

"What type of mileage would he get out of a suicide?"

"I wouldn't know. My neurons are connected differently than Czerny's. Of that I am sure."

Perhaps there was nothing more esoteric than ordinary academic politics that governed Professor Czerny's moves. I thought I shouldn't wait any longer to tell Professor Turner about my membership in the committee.

"Professor Czerny wants me to be on the committee. Since I was a bit confused ..."

I was about to inform him, while controlling my anxiety, that I had already agreed.

"Go for it," he said with enthusiasm that startled me. "Yes, go for it. You need some first hand experience with academic lunacy. It will help you when you start on your own teaching career. Who else is on the committee?"

"Professors Fuller, Baxter and Blackwell. Professor Fuller is the chairman."

"I could have guessed the composition of the committee."

"Really?"

"Fuller is a professor. Blackwell is an associate professor. It isn't official yet, but everybody knows that he will be given tenure and promoted soon. Baxter joined the department recently. It's a sort of balanced ticket."

I wanted to talk more about the committee members. I had sufficient judgment, however, to realize that I should quit while I was ahead. So I said that once I finished the experiment - the one I had been about to start that morning - I would go hiking with my son, Jay, to the spot he showed on the map. Well, that brought out the amicable man in Professor Turner and he advised me extensively, describing every slope and turn of the trail with great enthusiasm.

I was relieved that my membership on the committee did not irritate him. Indeed I was quite glad that we parted on friendly terms, talking about the great outdoors.

I was in the corridor, going back to my lab, when he yelled, "Good luck on the Chemistry Crime Committee."

Chapter 3

The Committee Meets

D r. Sankar!" I heard my name called from across the corridor. It was Cathy Quintaro's musical voice.

"You're a difficult man to get hold of," she said as we walked toward each other. "You don't have a phone. And I can't even find your desk."

"I know. You have to go through a real maze to get to it."

"Professor Fuller set the first meeting of the new committee for two-thirty this afternoon. He told me that I had to find you wherever you are and whatever you're doing and tell you that it's an important meeting and you can't miss it."

My time sense indicated it was one-thirty.

"You're off by a whole ten minutes! The time now is one-forty," Cathy announced when I told her my guess.

It would take more than fifty minutes to get anywhere with my experiment. The decisive experiment would have to wait for another day.

"I need a cup of coffee," I said.

"Come with me. We have a constant supply downstairs for the caffeine addicts"

As we walked toward the office I asked her about the vacant faculty position in the department.

"How many applied?"

"Two hundred showed interest. We now have more than a hundred and fifty completed files."

The slim chance I thought I had became even slimmer.

"Any idea when they are going to start reviewing the files."

"I don't really know. Linda next door handles that project. Evidently there was a committee. It was supposed to come up with a short list of the best applicants, but Professor Czerny abolished the committee."

"Why?"

"I haven't the faintest idea. I really don't understand how they do business in Chemistry. I only started working here about a month back. Before that I was a secretary in Hispanic Studies. Things were quite different there."

"Perhaps the dean told Professor Czerny to stop the search"

"That's not what I heard. Professor Czerny, Professor Fuller and a couple of other big shots in the department have been arguing with each other about the type of candidate they want."

"I thought that was all settled. The ad said they wanted an experimental physical chemist."

"I wouldn't know the difference between one chemist and the other. What I don't understand is why so many people want that job when they pay peanuts."

For some it is the glory of scientific fame. For others it is freedom to do what they want. For me it is simply a matter of finding a permanent home for my family before I need a cane to amble.

*   *   *

I knocked promptly at two-thirty on the partially opened door.

"Come right in," greeted Professor Fuller rising from his chair. "You're Sankar, right? Jim Fuller here. Just Jim."

I shook hands with the professor and immediately felt a tinge of self-reproach and pain. I had forgotten to use the American hand-shaking technique and let my hand flop in the Indian fashion while the professor shook it vigorously. Perhaps such differences in style do not always give an unfavorable impression, but you worry about every small detail when you have to impress the established elite so that you just might end up being the one chosen among the two hundred or more applicants.

"Why don't you have a seat and make yourself comfortable. The others are obviously not as punctual. But they'll be here sooner or later." With those words Professor Fuller went back to what he had been doing before I entered - examining a computer print-out and marking it with colored pencils.

Professor Fuller was very muscular and athletic. His thick hair was neatly brushed back giving prominence to his high temples. A bicycle hanging on the wall, next to the door, suggested the source of his well-maintained physique. The shelves in the room were crowded with neatly bound documents; the meager collection of books, scattered here and there, were undoubtedly relics from his student days. A few photographs of the professor socializing and shaking hands with celebrities - including one with a recent Nobel laureate of questionable accomplishments and unquestionable suavity - were hanging on the wall behind his chair.

I realized that I was in a precarious situation. I had no way of guessing when the meeting would actually start, each academic adhering to his own private standard time. I couldn't of course leave Professor Fuller's office without appearing rude. And if I waited there, like some one in a third world tea shop with no pressing engagements, I'd give a wrong impression of myself. A dynamic individual - the only type they employ in the research dominated universities - would not just sit there waiting for something to happen. He would be on the go every minute, spewing out new ideas, examining the computer screen, carrying out experiments or browsing in current journals with a critical eye. What was I to do then? I was quite relieved when I spied a stack of recent issues of *Science* on Professor Fuller's bookshelf.

"Do you have the third issue for November?" I inquired as though there was something special in it. Professor Fuller passed the whole stack silently. I did some serious browsing for what felt like an eternity. Professor Fuller better believe it, I was in control of my destiny and never at a loss for things to do.

I had begun to wonder whether the meeting would ever start when a sloppily dressed man entered the office. He was probably thirty-ish but his hairline had already receded several inches. His sneakers had seen better days, as had his profusely wrinkled grey slacks and pale blue shirt. The twinkle in his blue eyes drew attention away from the crumpled appearance.

"Is this the Ad Hoc committee?" he asked.

"It most certainly is. What brings you here, Fred?"

"I happen to be one of the members."

"Really? I don't see your honorable name here."

"That's because I'm Professor Blackwell's replacement. He couldn't or wouldn't be on the committee. So the head pointed his finger at me and said, 'You're it'."

"What was Blackwell's excuse?"

"I haven't the vaguest idea, Jim"

"Blackwell is not on any committee now, is he?"

"I don't know."

"You know, Fred, that's unfair. I think each of us should share the departmental chores equally."

"I agree with you, Jim. I agree with you two hundred and fifty per cent."

"I know Rich has been working very hard on his research. I always said that we must encourage research productivity, particularly among the junior faculty. But now that Rich is well established and has a thriving research group, he must be asked to spend more time on departmental duties. I know it isn't as much fun, but we must all do our share. I'll talk to Czerny about it."

"I can't agree with you more, Jim," the newcomer said and turned toward me, extending his hand. "You must be the post-doc on the committee. Fred Findlay."

I introduced myself and remembered to give a firm hand shake this time.

Professor Fuller continued the comments on Richard Blackwell. "Fred, did you know that Rich was recommended for tenure. I've no doubt he will get it."

"Yes. But being the low man on the departmental totem pole, I heard the news just yesterday."

"Rich has an impressive file. He has published nearly forty papers in the last two years. Right now he has a group of ten grad students and grants for almost half a million dollars."

"Very impressive."

"I've been at this place for over twenty five years. I think this is the first time tenure was recommended for anyone in four years."

Nearly forty papers in two years! Half a million dollars in grants! That was indeed an impressive performance. I was depressed when I thought what it meant for my future prospects in academe. I had been having a difficult time coming up on anyone's short list of candidates for an assistant professorship. Nevertheless I had been dreaming of landing a beginning faculty position in some university one day. It seemed to me, at that moment, that reaching the next step of securing a tenured appointment might be far beyond my reach.

"Fred, I'm curious about your thoughts on this matter," Professor Fuller continued. "You know Blackwell's work better than I do. How much of his work, in your opinion, is really fundamental? How much of it just happens to be a passing fad? It looks to me as though the rate at which Richard publishes - let's leave the question of quality aside - implies a safe and well-worn area of research. Maybe refinements of what has essentially been done by others. You see what I mean?"

"Well, I really don't know," Professor Findlay was slow in answering. "Blackwell and I use similar instruments. But beyond that we've nothing in common. I can't really comment on his work."

"I'll grant you that there certainly is need for highly active and visible scientists. We need people who keep stirring the pot, get glaring publicity, attract oodles of grant money and recruit scores of grad students. Otherwise we'll all be dead, right? We have to keep moving, be dynamic, just to survive. But I also think that most of the fundamental research gets done by less visible researchers with modest budgets and fewer publications. Don't you agree?"

I was thoroughly puzzled by the conversation. They were discussing privileged information before me, a post-doc who wouldn't be allowed into faculty meetings. I couldn't have been completely invisible. Was I supposed to step out of the room while the two professors debated the merits of Professor Blackwell's research?

I was also puzzled by Professor Fuller's attitude. He was a high-ranking member of the faculty. Had he objected to the quality of research, Professor Blackwell would not have been recommended for tenure without an extensive review of his articles. Why hadn't he raised his doubts before?

The conversation continued for another few minutes when Professor Fuller looked at his wrist watch, expressed dismay and dialed the phone. "Hi ... I thought so ... We've been waiting for ages."

A minute later a stocky man in western boots crashed through the half-open door and collapsed into a chair. He smelled like a barrel of ash trays. It was obviously Professor Niles Baxter.

"So here we are – in the Chemistry Crime Committee. Let's begin, gentlemen," he said.

"I resent your attitude, Niles. This is not a Crime Committee and I wish you at least get the name right." Professor Fuller said, distinctly pronouncing each word.

"That's what the grad students are saying."

"What?"

"I heard a couple of guys in the hall."

"How the hell did the students get a whiff?"

I thought it was wise to keep quiet.

"Beats me," Niles Baxter said

"We may as well do so," Professor Fuller agreed, as he pulled his chair around the desk. The four of us were now sitting without anything between us, our legs almost touching at the center. "First let me point out to the non-faculty member on the committee that we're very happy to have him with us. For a very long time I've been advocating - without any support from the powers above - appointment of post-doctoral personnel to academic committees."

"It's a very good idea," Professor Findlay commented.

"They do it in every other university," Professor Baxter added.

"We here are a bit behind the times," Professor Fuller said.

"Things are improving though," Professor Findlay said.

"Now for the business at hand," the chairman said in a raised voice. "I assume that everyone knows why we're here. Briefly, a sample of cyanide reacted with a grad student. The result of the chemical reaction was very unpleasant. And we, as a committee, are asked to look into the human side of this tragic reaction. Here are extra copies of Czerny's memo, in case you forgot to bring yours."

"Is it a unimolecular or bimolecular reaction? In other words, is it a suicide or homicide?" Professor Baxter looked pleased with his phrasing.

"The police haven't closed the books on the case yet, but there is no doubt it is suicide."

"You certain about that?"

"As certain as one can be. The point is, Niles, a suicide raises questions about our programs. Homicide - very unlikely as I understand - does not concern us. So we may as well be cautious and proceed assuming it was indeed suicide."

"Should we then call this the Suicide Committee?" Professor Baxter added.

Professor Fuller looked irritated but didn't say anything. No one spoke for a while.

"The committee has a broad mandate," Professor Fuller went on. "We can, if we so desire, investigate every aspect of this unfortunate incident. But we all know that's impractical - quite impractical - even if Niles gets here on time . . . I must make at least one nasty comment on Niles' tardiness."

Professor Fuller chuckled at his own comments before continuing and Professor Baxter looked disgusted.

"The question then is this. On what areas should we focus our attention?"

There was a moment's silence while we looked at each other.

"Why don't we wait for the police statement and then write a hundred page report concurring? That's the sort of thing Czerny likes," Professor Baxter suggested. He too was pleased at his own wit and laughed loudly. No one joined him.

"I agree that there's some merit to that idea... But honestly, Niles, I'd like to have some seriousness in the proceedings," Professor Fuller said sternly.

There was an uneasy silence for a few moments until Professor Findlay commented in a quiet voice. "I'm at a loss what any committee can do at this stage. This business seems to be something that should concern the police . . . not us. If and when the police report raises questions regarding departmental policies we should discuss them."

"Fred, you just verbalized a common misunderstanding."

"Yes?"

"What would happen if the number of grad students in each lab decreased, say, by 20 percent?"

"It would be a disaster," replied Professor Findlay

"I don't see how I could carry out my research program. I'm barely surviving with a minimum number," said Professor Baxter.

"Besides that, you and I would have to do the undergrad lab courses. We would lose whatever meager time we have for keeping up with the developments in our respective fields," Professor Fuller continued. "It goes without saying that no major university can survive without a healthy number of grad students. Indeed I'm going to be very bold and say that the difference between us and Harvard is the quality and quantity of grad students. And nothing else."

"No one argues on that matter, Jim. That's why I've been advocating aggressive recruiting techniques and twenty-five per cent increase in stipends. Leave Harvard out of the picture. We aren't even competing with other departments around us." Professor Baxter became very animated as he talked.

"Yes, we have to move in that direction. But before the dean coughs up the money for such improvements we have to hold the fort, if I may mix metaphors. This committee's true purpose is to find out the impact of the suicide on our efforts to keep a first class graduate program going."

I scribbled on my note pad quickly: *How does suicide affect grad programs at the U?*

"What impact? Are you telling me that the grad students are going to stop doing research because some idiot swallowed cyanide and killed himself?"

"You are missing the point, Niles ... by miles. A suicide means pressure, anger, frustration and many other ugly things. We should find out what's happening to the grad students. Find ways of improving their lives a bit - not out of altruism - but for the sake of our own careers."

"Sure, sure. You want grad students and I want grad students. Our survival depends on them. And we want to do the best we can to get them and to hold on to them until they produce some publishable data. But I don't see what the hell this committee can do other than waste time. And people like me, without tenure, working with the most out-dated equipment and the least prepared grad students, can't afford it." Professor Baxter looked straight at Professor Fuller as he spoke.

A few moments of uneasy silence followed before Professor Fuller reasserted himself.

"I was afraid of this type of beginning and I didn't want us to spend weeks defining our role. So I sketched a set of goals for the committee. I've been hoping that we'd have an intelligent debate and come up with a consensus. But since Niles is bent on acting stupid - I'm sorry but I have to be blunt - let me present my ideas and see where we can go from there. Believe me, I really hate to impose my ideas on others. I'd prefer dialogue and consensus any day."

Professor Fuller looked around but no one commented.

"The first thing we should do is to find out whether Gregg Westover - that I believe was the name of the student - was under any undue pressure. This can be ascertained by talking to a handful people in the department who knew Gregg well. Sankar, I think you have a better chance of accomplishing this task than anyone else here. You are relatively new to the department. Besides people are more relaxed with post-docs than with the faculty."

Professor Fuller paused and looked around. Again the three of us kept quiet.

"Do I take it then that's an acceptable activity for the committee? Speak now or hold your peace until I retire."

The other two professors agreed in muffled voices.

"Sankar, you think you can do that?"

"Yes, I'd like to. Whom should I talk to?"

"Check with Martha Gwinn first. She's the secretary who takes care of graduate student affairs. She's very good and knows who hangs out with whom."

"What exactly am I looking for?"

"Was Gregg under any undue academic pressure?" Professor Fuller repeated with a touch of impatience. "People might tell you if Gregg had been bad mouthing the department, if he talked about killing himself because of what goes on in the department. We like to find out about such things before others do."

"Should I report my findings to you?"

"Yes. Please do."

Pressures on Gregg W? Talk to staff, grad students and faculty.

"Jim, this may the appropriate time to bring up an important point," Professor Findlay said.

"What is it, Fred?"

"I understand that Gregg was fired from his job last week."

"I heard something to that effect. I am not sure about the details."

"How could that be?" Professor Baxter joined. "Don't the grad students have contracts from September to June?"

"They usually do. But Gregg was a special case and Czerny was pretty mad at him for some reason or other. As I said, I don't know the details."

"I wonder whether being fired in mid-year might have contributed to suicide," I said and immediately wished I hadn't. I wanted to be a silent observer and not an active participant.

"If so, Czerny would be in trouble, I mean serious trouble. That explains why we have this committee in the first place. We will be meeting until we come up with a lengthy report exonerating our fearless leader," Professor Baxter was quick to respond.

Was Professor Czerny sticking his neck out, according to the motto he had professed, by firing an employee without due process? I wondered.

"Niles, your comments are uncalled for," Professor Fuller scolded. "We really don't know what Czerny actually did. We could, of course, ask him to make a statement to this committee at an appropriate time. Meanwhile, Sankar, you should put into your equation the effects of sudden unemployment."

"Yes I will. One thing puzzles me though. I was talking to Professor Turner, who was Gregg's supervisor. He didn't say anything about the firing. He should have been informed by Professor Czerny"

"Frank Turner doesn't care what happens to his grad students," Professor Fuller said abruptly. "He has the worst cavalier attitude when it comes to directing students and training them into researchers. Indeed, I believe his attitude exerted more pressure on Gregg than temporary unemployment. I will, of course, suspend my judgment until Sankar's investigation is done."

I was looking in the direction of Professor Findlay then. He made a face as though warning me. Odd, I thought.

"A good research advisor should be very firm while giving the usual tea and sympathy. Frank, I'm afraid, fails on both counts. I'd like to devote a part of the next meeting to discussing how a research advisor's attitude puts an undue burden on his grad students."

Professor Findlay was still looking at me in a strange fashion. I wondered why.

"We are spending too much time on one item," Professor Fuller continued. "Let's move on to the next. This is about the faculty perception. We must find out how the faculty feels about this incident. I don't recall the name of the university in the East. It had been a third rate place for a very long time. Then the faculty in chemistry took a survey and came up with something like twelve commandments on how to treat the graduate students. The grad student enrollment has been going up and evidently they're also getting a better bunch. I think we now have an opportunity to find out what our faculty think and what we can do to make this university more attractive to the students out there... Fred you're a diplomat, in the best sense of the word. Can you direct your efforts in this direction?"

Prof. Findlay to survey faculty on grad student-faculty relations.

"Yes, but we have to talk about the details."

"You and I can go through the details later.... Last but not the least. Czerny appointed this committee and he should come up with some money for secretarial time and long-distance calls. We can take this opportunity to survey how our grad student stipends and facilities compare with those at other similar institutions. We can use that information to upgrade our programs and, maybe, even to find ways of aggressively recruiting grad students. Honest to God, we need better students and more of them."

"Wasn't I saying that?" interjected Professor Baxter and looked toward Professor Findlay for support.

"Maybe. But you had no plan. You didn't even see how a committee could be effective in such matters."

"I had a plan, a very specific one. It didn't need a committee."

"I have to disagree with you, Niles. A vague dream is not a plan. At any rate since you are so concerned about this issue why don't I put you in the driver's seat. Call a few of our competitors and find out what they are paying grad students and how they are recruiting them."

Prof. Baxter to survey grad student stipends, etc.

The meeting became incoherent after that. I couldn't tell whether the professors were arguing or agreeing with each other. At any rate I felt that my presence was not required. After looking attentive for a few minutes, as each of them talked, I got up and waited for Professor Fuller to notice me.

"Sankar, I see you have to go. Actually we are finished with the business for the day. Same time next week?"

I nodded assent and started to leave.

"Sankar," Professor Fuller called. "Talk to as many people as you can. If there is a perception among graduate students that any faculty member is nasty and mean, above and beyond the call of duty, we want to know. We can't afford to let a few unconcerned professors ruin a first rate graduate program."

Professor Fuller called out before I closed the door behind me.

"Another important point, Sankar. We are not playing cops. Your mission is strictly limited. It is to find out how Gregg's ghost is likely to affect the academic atmosphere in the department. None of us have the authority to do police work or even contact the police. Only David - Professor Czerny - will deal with the police."

*   *   *

It occurred to me, the moment I left Professor Fuller's office, that I might be able to find out more from him about the advertised faculty position in the department. I didn't want to go back while the two other professors were still in conference with Professor Fuller and so I paced the corridors for about fifteen minutes waiting for the opportune moment.

"Well, it turns out that we have an extra factor to consider now," Professor Fuller said when I brought up the question. "The Board of Higher Ed has been putting pressure on the president to hire more women and minorities. Not your type but the under-represented type - Hispanics, African-Americans and Native-Americans. And the university administration has been holding back funds unless we show, before we go ahead with the interviews, that there is a good chance of hiring a minority or a woman faculty member. So the question before the faculty now is whether we can broaden the definition of a physical chemist to include minorities in the pool. All I can say at this juncture, Sankar, is that there is a fierce debate going on among the chemistry faculty and I don't know what the outcome is likely to be."

"I applied three months back, soon after the ad appeared in the *Chemical and Engineering News*."

"That's a long time."

"I'm curious about my chances."

"We haven't begun screening the files yet. So I'm afraid I can't tell you much about your chances or anybody's. But I can tell you something about the process of selection. Don't stand there. Have a seat."

I knew then that the explanation was going to be a long one. Professor Fuller looked thoughtful for a long time before proceeding. "When we hire new faculty, Sankar, we follow the same guidelines we will be using six years down the road when the candidates come up for tenure. We look for outstanding accomplishments in three areas – teaching, research and service. The applicants for an assistant professorship do not usually have any teaching experience, unless you count their stints as teaching assistants. So teaching wouldn't be an appropriate criterion for selection. As for the research, we usually get our readings from the professors under whom the candidate did his or her work.

"The service part is tricky. The main part of a faculty member's service would be service to the department in the form of committee work, advising, recruiting grad students and, in general, improving the conditions under which we must all toil. There is no way of judging the temperament of a candidate before we hire him or her. Would the candidate be a good cooperative citizen of the department? Or would he be a constant pain in the prominent parts, like Niles?

"In your particular case, you have an opportunity to demonstrate your potential for service to the department through your work with the committee. In the weeks to come this committee will be dealing with several vital issues that are peripherally related to the grad student's suicide. These are issues that concern every member of the department. So you will have opportunities to show your talents in the area of inter-personal relations. And when we're ready to seriously consider the candidates for the faculty position in this department, we'll have to take into account your committee work. That may very well give you the needed extra points."

I thanked Professor Fuller as I left. There was a time when I had dreamed of discovering a great scientific principle and being rewarded by a professorship in a prestigious university. Later, there was a time when I had hoped that I'd be able to collect massive data in some area and be recompensed with a faculty position in a good university. More recently I had been praying that the competence I had showed in research would get me a foothold, and adequate remuneration, in any one of the universities in this land of plenty. Now, as I understood from Professor Fuller, it would be service and inter-personal relations that could boost my chances. I would have preferred to be judged by what I had accomplished in the lab, but if writing memos and getting along with the members of the committee would give me a chance to secure a faculty position, I'd do that too. I was in no position to dictate my own terms.

*   *   *

"Just now you came home?" Meera said using *Telugu* syntax as I walked into our town house through the sliding back door.

She was sitting in front of the computer - a machine of outdated capacities that we bought for a song. I had told her earlier that I was planning to do an experiment that could keep me quite late in the lab. I didn't want to disturb what she was doing by going over my day's activities just then.

"Where is Jay?" I asked. I thought he and I could go for tennis, leaving Meera to finish her work.

Meera answered in *Telugu*. Since I wasn't expected home before supper, she had given Jay permission to visit a friend and go to the Cub Scout den meeting directly from there.

"Are you needing some coffee?" Meera asked.

That was a literal translation of a Telugu expression: *"meeku kafi kavala?"*

I knew she would start moving toward the kitchen unless I stopped her, so I said I had to study an important article and went upstairs. Meera, I was certain, was aware that I had told a harmless lie so that she could continue what she had been doing. Once upstairs, I thought about the different ways the two of us had learned to use English.

I came to the United States, eight years ahead of Meera, as a graduate student. It became clear to me soon that unless I wanted to permanently settle into the life of a lab technician, taking hourly instructions from superiors, I had to improve my command of English. Fortunately I had a unique opportunity to better my language skills. My first roommate in the graduate student dorm was a fifty year old Polish Jew, with the anglicized name of Joseph Birk, who worshiped the language of Shakespeare and Conrad. He was then writing a thesis on philosophy of science and told me, on more than one occasion, that it was his competence in English that gave him the slim chance to make a living with dignity. It was Joseph who provided the inspiration and instruction for improving my English.

Since he was one of those teachers who made every criticism feel like a compliment, I learned quickly and with pleasure, even though I could not come to Joseph's level. I began writing with care and speaking with proper syntax, most of the time. Being in constant contact with English speaking post-docs, profs and graduate students gave me the chance to practice what Joseph taught. At the time of my doctoral thesis defense, one of the professors commented on my abilities to write well.

"I think the British did a damn good job in India," another professor commented. I was too worried about the exam to thank Joseph or to point out that the British influence had waned from India before it reached the tiny hamlets of Andhra Pradesh.

After I had my doctorate, I returned to India for a visit and married according to my mother's wishes. It was, of course, an arranged marriage between two with matching horoscopes. Meera joined me in the United States a few months later.

I was pleasantly surprised to find, soon after we were introduced, that Meera had a good command of the English language. I realized later, however, that she speaks three different versions of the language. If we were in company of American friends she would have said, "Coffee, Sankar?"

When we are alone she used literal translations of Telugu expressions as she did just now. During those times she will not address me by my name which, back home, is considered to be the proper etiquette for wives.

When she is irritated with me and wants to win a one-sided argument she resorts to march of gerunds. Thus if I had requested coffee and she was upset about something I have done, she would say, "You are wanting coffee. I am wanting to make coffee. But how am I to do when the kitchen is so small and you are not even making good salary?"

There is yet another dialect she uses exclusively in the company of ladies from Andhra Pradesh. In this dialect all nouns are from English and all verbs from Telugu and the rest of the words freely chosen from either language.

As I was thinking about these matters, Meera finished her work on the computer. She called from downstairs: "I am making coffee now."

She said that in Telugu.

I went downstairs. "No coffee but..." I moved closer and said, "Jay is not going to be back for another two hours. Since you are done with your work for now..."

"You think you are telling me something I don't understand?" Meera said in English with pretended seriousness.

After that there was no reason to talk in English or Telugu.

Chapter 4

Gregg Westover's Graduate Studies

I bicycled with Jay to Chavez Elementary School as I usually did on school days, and then turned around toward the university campus. Meera and I had worried that changing schools in the middle of the year would cause Jay troubles. To our great relief, he adjusted well to the new school in Gadsden. In fact, he was more enthusiastic about it than the one he had attended in New Jersey.

The bike route went through a quiet neighborhood from which auto traffic was all but absent. As I pedaled, the dogs looked through their respective fences, some mournfully and others barking or yelping excitedly, and the cats examined me from their vantage points on windowsills or walked unconcerned amidst the bushes. The road was flat, the jagged edges of the mountains stood on the distant horizon, leaving most of the city as level as an optical bench, so flat that I could pedal without much exertion even on my three-speed Schwinn, undoubtedly the slowest and heaviest bicycle in Gadsden. As I sat upright and gently pushed the pedals down, other cyclists with their rumps in the air raced past me on both sides, their machines making swishing sounds like arrows from a taut bow, speeding to their sure destination. I prefer the slow ride with my head above my shoulders, because it allows me to think of what has happened or to plan the day ahead.

Over the years, I have come to the conclusion that faculty are a bunch of anarchists held together by their dire need to find grad students. It is no secret that a professor's professional standing depends on his research productivity. And productivity depends, in today's experimental and computer-centered sciences, on the number of graduate students under one's tutelage and the hours each of them spends in the laboratory.

The professors were obviously worried that the suicide in a lab might reflect adversely on the academic atmosphere in the department. It might make it harder for them to recruit new grad students or even to keep those who were already there from leaving the department. If they knew the circumstances behind the suicide, they could come up with a strategy to minimize its possible negative effects.

Granted they had reasons to worry, why did they want a post-doc to investigate the circumstances that led Gregg to swallow poison? Was it because a post-doc, not being a member of the faculty, might be trusted to be more objective? Or was it because a post-doc could be talked into coming up with the report the faculty really wanted?

Why was I specifically chosen? At least thirty post-docs wandered the corridors of the department, every one of them more familiar with the department than I. While I doubted that the committee could achieve anything useful, I also felt—at the same time—elated at being the one chosen. Since my boss, Professor Turner, had not been consulted, it was obvious that Professor Czerny had chosen me for some qualities other than expertise in a research area. Very likely he asked one of the secretaries to give him all the post-doc files, and while he was browsing through them, something about me must have struck him as unique or interesting. If that were indeed the case, I had managed to attract the attention of the head of the department and, in a sense, to get a foot in the door of the exclusive faculty club. And my contribution as a committee member might just buy me the much-needed goodwill, as Professors Czerny and Fuller had indicated. It was indeed a happy thought.

In that state of optimism, a plan took root in my mind. What I had to do was write an authoritative report, very much like the research proposals I had composed before. I could visualize the outline of the report and its subtitles.

Recent Tragedy

Statement of the Problem

Perception of the Staff

Perception of the Graduate Students

Perception of the Faculty

Is the Problem Real?

Recommendations

It was indeed time to begin interviews. I lifted myself above the saddle and pedaled hard to speed up the sluggish bike.

*   *   *

I was told that Martha Gwinn, the elderly woman in the chemistry-office complex, took care of every matter that concerned graduate students in our department. She warned them of the graduate college rules, reminded them of the departmental deadlines, consoled them when they needed sympathy by telling about the experiences of previous grad students, and, in general, kept an eye on each of them. Her desk was my first stop.

She was sipping her morning coffee and doing a crossword puzzle as I walked into the office. I didn't have to introduce myself; she spoke with a welcoming smile: "Dr. Sankar! You came to talk to me about Gregg Westover."

"Yes, indeed. How did you know?"

"Professor Fuller called yesterday as I was closing shop. He told me to give you all the help I could."

I didn't know whether to be amused or surprised. I was having difficulty taking the committee seriously, even though I had come to the conclusion that it might serve some useful function and—more importantly—help my career. Professor Fuller, on the other hand, seemed to have a messianic zeal about the committee. He was bent upon seeing that its work proceeded with clockwork precision.

"Did you know Gregg well?" I asked her, leaning on the filing cabinet next to the door.

"Not really. He kept to himself."

"No close friends?"

"I'm not aware of any. He roomed with John Spikes, another of our graduate students, during his first semester here. After that I understand he lived alone. Probably John could tell you more about him than I can."

"Tell me whatever you know about Gregg, please."

"Some students talk to me about their personal problems. I suppose they think I'm more sympathetic than the profs. But Gregg never said anything about himself or his family or friends. He was a loner. So I know nothing about him other than his academic standing."

"How is ... *was* he as a graduate student?"

"He wasn't doing well. His grades were pretty bad, Dr. Sankar. I didn't think he would be able to jump all the hurdles to get a degree at our university."

Gregg had gotten a BS with less than a B average from an unknown college in Texas, as I found from the files Martha Gwinn handed me. It took him nearly six years to finish the minimum required courses. Following graduation, he worked for three years as an insurance investigator in Louisiana. He then returned to university life as a graduate student in chemistry. His first attempts at Guadalupe University had not been particularly successful; he failed the PhD qualifying exams twice and after five years got a master's degree instead, something most students complete in two years. It was indeed a dismal academic record.

"How did he ever get admitted into our program with a record like that?" I asked.

"I couldn't figure that out, Dr. Sankar. At first the faculty committee rejected his application. He got the lowest score from everyone on the committee. I was about to send the standard rejection letter when Professor Fuller asked me, at the very last moment, to hold back. A couple of months later, Professor Czerny told me to send Gregg a one-year contract."

"A contract?"

"A teaching assistantship for a year."

"Very puzzling."

"That's what I thought."

Why did Professors Czerny and Fuller circumvent the normal process of selecting students for graduate study? Had they known of some special qualities that indicated a greater potential than his grades? During my meetings with them, the two professors had not mentioned being particularly familiar with Gregg's background. On the contrary, I got the impression that Gregg meant no more to them than any of the other faceless grad students who toiled in the ivory tower.

"Did you know about the letter Professor Czerny recently sent to Gregg? I understand his employment was terminated abruptly."

"I heard about it, but I didn't see the letter."

"Don't you get a copy for your files?"

"It's unusual to fire someone in the middle of the year. Actually it's never happened before, in all the years I've worked at the U. Since it's so unusual, Professor Czerny sent the letter and documentation to the dean. The dean's office picked up the matter from there. They haven't sent us a copy yet."

"When did they mail the letter?"

"According to Jane in the dean's office, it was forwarded to the provost's office. She doesn't know the current status of the file."

"So Gregg may or may not have gotten the letter of termination."

"That's what I figured, Dr. Sankar."

"Is it possible that he got the letter and killed himself in despair?"

"Hard to tell ... but I don't think so."

"Why do you say that?"

"He wasn't the type. I can't say why I feel that way."

"It's hard to tell what makes someone flip."

"True. There's something else that puzzles me about him. He came to my office on Friday, the day before ... you know. He came to borrow the education college booklet. He was more cheerful than I had ever seen him."

As I gathered from Martha Gwinn, Gregg was planning to drop out of grad school and go for a teaching certificate. He thought he could be done with most of the necessary courses by the end of summer and do his practice teaching in one of the junior-highs next Fall. Evidently there was a great demand for junior-high teachers in the small towns in the western states. If being fired in the middle of the year bothered Gregg, he did a good job of hiding it.

"He also told me that he would be getting enough money to put a hefty down payment on a ranch house."

"Inheritance?"

"He didn't say."

Martha Gwinn, the thoughtful woman, had made me copies of all the important papers in Gregg's file. I could see that her reputation as a helpful and efficient secretary was well deserved..

I thanked her as I left the office. Later I scribbled the following in my notebook.

Tuesday 8:30 A. M.

On Friday before suicide G was very cheerful & optimistic when he talked to MG. (Morning or afternoon?) Did he receive the termination letter later that day? Could that letter have anything to with his suicide? It looks unlikely since he was planning to move on. Besides, he inherited a bit of wealth which should have kept his spirits high.

*   *   *

I had checked into Professor Turner's laboratory during the second week of December. Fall semester had ended, except for a few final exams; the campus was sleepy and the chemistry building appeared empty. I was assigned a small, overstuffed room on the fourth floor for both lab and office, and that satisfied me since I'd be the only occupant. Professor Turner's main lab was at the opposite corner of the building on the same floor.

On the very first day I came to work Professor Turner took me to his main lab for an introduction to his research group. By modern standards, my boss had a very small group: two grad students, one undergrad and me. The undergraduate, a tall thin woman called Rhoda, was freaking-out – in her own words – since she had to prepare for a final exam in Physics scheduled for next day. I offered my help as a tutor, should she need one. One of the grad students was from Korea and spoke so softly I couldn't make out what he was saying. Professor Turner explained that Kim was about to go back to Korea to be with his dying father and would be back later. The other grad student was Greg Westover; Professor Turner was generous to me in his introduction and spent a good deal of time telling Gregg about my background and my accomplishments, as he called them.

A six-footer, Gregg was on the heavy side, with neck-length blonde hair that hung ruler straight. Professor Turner asked him to show me around the campus, introduce me to the service personnel in glass-blowing, electronics lab, machine shop, etc. It's hard to get research done these days unless you have the hearty cooperation of the service personnel, so I was hoping for enthusiastic introductions, very much like what Professor Turner had done. Gregg, unfortunately, had a different style. At our first stop, the machine shop, he looked vaguely in the direction of a mechanic and said, "This is the new guy in Turner's lab." Subsequent introductions weren't any better. Gregg looked bored and even irritated during the half an hour he spent showing me around. I attributed his disposition to the end-of-the-semester blues.

A few days later, I went to visit Gregg in Professor Turner's main lab. It was time for me to get acquainted with the research interests of the other members of the group. Gregg's desk was next to the double doors into the lab, facing the wall. On his left side, between the desk and the corner, was a four-foot wide bookshelf packed with reference books and company catalogs. Beyond the bookshelf, on the wall running perpendicular, there was a small partially-opened door. Professor Turner had explained that it led to a common room, actually a long narrow corridor converted into an annex, used by several research groups to store their older files.

"I'm not doing anything now," Gregg said when I asked him about his research. He was sitting at his desk looking at the sports section of a newspaper.

I was surprised at the abruptness of his statement. I didn't know then that Gregg had been in graduate school for some time; I thought he was a first year student, still finding his way around a research lab. I said, "It takes a while to get started on a research project."

"Particularly, if you work for Turner."

I waited for him to elaborate on the statement.

"He has an out-dated mentality. He thinks that a grad student must do everything. Design the apparatus, make the compounds, write original software and do every measurement. Other profs let their students work together on research projects. Sometimes two or three students write their theses on the same topic from different angles."

I didn't want to get into a debate with Gregg so I remained silent.

"Now Professor T wants me to learn organic chemistry and make a couple of obscure compounds, and I don't know beans about synthesis."

"Maybe I could help. Over the years I've synthesized a few difficult compounds."

"I'll think about it."

Gregg seemed to be unenthusiastic about the project. Since he showed no inclination to continue the conversation, I said, "I'll be seeing you," as I got up. He remained silent. I couldn't guess whether he was having a bad day or was just a secretive person, troubled by company. During the Christmas break I saw him few times in the corridors of chemistry building, now almost empty; he showed no sign of recognizing me.

Remembering that one meeting I had had with Gregg, I wrote down in my notebook:

Was Gregg's reluctance to have anything to do with me a sign of some sort of depression? Was he normally uncommunicative, without a safety valve for emotional swings?

*   *   *

I noticed, looking at Gregg's file, that Conrad Seely was one of the professors who had written a letter of appraisal from Guadalupe. Conrad and I had collaborated on a project and published a paper together several years earlier when he and I were both working as post-docs in the same department. A stocky person with an enormous head, Conrad used to wander about in the lab with a coffee cup permanently implanted to his right hand. I called him long-distance to find out about Gregg's life before he came to our university.

"Still a post-doc, eh?" Conrad asked

"Unfortunately."

"Don't say that. It isn't very comfortable being a faculty member."

"Really?"

"Yeah. We got a new head of the department last semester, a real jerk. He says that any faculty member who doesn't pull in at least a hundred thousand dollar grant a year won't be considered for raises from now on."

Conrad told me that the pressure to bring in research money was so oppressive that he was looking for a job elsewhere. After letting him talk for a few minutes about his troubles at Guadalupe, I introduced Gregg into the conversation.

"That guy! I don't remember what I wrote. Couldn't have been all that good."

"It was pretty bad. You said that you wouldn't have him in your lab."

"That's right. Gregg was one of our least desirable grad students."

"Did he work with you?"

"No. But his reputation was widespread. He didn't do much by way of research. He was always looking for short cuts to success. A term paper he wrote turned out to be a perfect copy of a section in a standard textbook. For his thesis, he lifted a couple of data tables from a well-known article by one of my friends. Unluckily for him, I found out before it was too late. The committee told him to do more work and rewrite the thesis without, of course, borrowing other people's data so freely. That was the worst graduate committee I ever served on."

"You should have expelled him from the university."

"That's what I'd have done. Unfortunately you have to follow lengthy, interminable procedures. Besides, his thesis director was up in arms when the suggestion was made. He thought that Gregg, crooked or not, was indispensable in the lab. You know, Sankar, that's the real problem with grad studies now. A professor, as long as he finds a student useful in his lab, even for dish washing, will defend him, her or it until kingdom come. The old days when the student planned and did the work independently are gone. You can't judge anyone objectively any more."

The letter Conrad wrote to Gadsden was very negative but did not mention Greggs's plagiarism. I asked him why.

"Then I'd have had to explain why we didn't expel him. I couldn't have said we, in the department here, didn't have the guts."

Gregg, like many grad students, had been employed by the University of

Gadsden as a teaching assistant - a TA. His duties were to supervise undergraduate lab work, grade home work and lab reports and conduct sundry discussions in the freshman courses. He was expected to spend nearly twenty hours a week doing these chores and was paid a half-time salary. He was also expected to devote the rest of his time to research under a professor or to graduate courses that would prepare him for research. Even though a TA is paid only for teaching, an assistantship is not considered to be employment; it is understood to be a partial scholarship that allows the student to advance his or her career and, by something akin to symbiosis, the supervisor's as well. Hence selection for a teaching assistantship is almost always based entirely on the candidate's potential for doing research and completing the doctoral program.

"I can't figure out why they offered Gregg a teaching assistantship here. None of the letters were complementary."

"I was surprised when I heard that Gregg had been offered an assistantship at your place. I thought you people had better luck getting grad students than we do. We have to practically scrape the bottom of the barrel.... Why are you asking me all these questions?" Conrad wanted to know.

"I didn't tell you, did I? Gregg committed suicide last Saturday."

"He committed suicide!"

"Yes. That's what I was told."

"Why? Why did he do that?"

"I wish I knew." I told Conrad why I was interested in Gregg and what I'd found out about him from Martha Gwinn.

"Gregg always saw the negative side of people, Sankar. Maybe after years of that he started seeing the negative side of himself which, I'm sure, would have been unbearable. If you start hating people, you end up hating yourself," Conrad theorized.

"That's a better explanation than any I can come up with."

"Talking about the negative side, I remember something else unpleasant about Gregg," Conrad said. "He was in the blackmailing business."

"Really?"

Jerry MacDonald - a chemistry professor *sans* tenure - was having an affair with an undergraduate student and Gregg found out about it. At that time MacDonald was under consideration for tenure. Gregg presented the evidence to Brenda MacDonald and threatened to show it to the dean. Brenda knew that this could ruin her husband's career and paid for Gregg's silence. It turned out that MacDonald didn't get tenure anyway - his grantsmanship not being aggressive enough to suit the department. The marriage hadn't been on a secure footing to begin with and the MacDonalds had a very difficult time coping with each other once he was denied tenure. They separated after bitter quarrels, but not before Brenda gave Jerry a list of sacrifices she had made for his career, among them the blackmail money she had paid to Gregg. Jerry was furious when he heard about it and wanted the head of the department to fire Gregg then and there, but the head said he would not get involved in personal affairs.

"I tell you, Sankar, there were too many troubling things about this guy." I wondered how much of this history was relevant to my investigation.

9:45 AM

Extremely poor academic record. How did G get into U of G grad school? Check again with Martha Gwinn.

Plagiarism. Blackmail. Would someone with such antisocial behavior turn hatred against himself?

Chapter 5

Ways of the Profs

During the first semester in our department, Gregg took a few courses and did no research. This was not unusual since the students often needed background courses before stepping into the lab. During the second semester, the spring semester, he started working in Professor Blackwell's laboratory but left at the end of the following summer to join Professor Turner's group. That was quite unusual. Switching supervisors before completing a project is a serious breach of faith. It also creates very bad feelings between the faculty members, which could be the beginning of troubles for the graduate student. Any student who changes advisors, quickly or casually, also gets into serious trouble with the administration. Because of this possibility, a student who can't get along with his supervisor will usually go to another department or to a different university to continue his studies rather than look for a different supervisor in the same department. Hence I was surprised that there was no explanation in Gregg's file about why he changed supervisors.

10:00 A. M.

Why Blackwell → Turner? What were the profs feelings?

*   *   *

I had been anxious to meet Professor Blackwell ever since I heard about his dramatic rise into the ranks of almost tenured faculty. Now that I knew he had been Gregg's research supervisor, albeit for only a semester and a summer, I felt I had a very good excuse to visit him.

"I made it perfectly clear to Czerny that I do not want to have anything to do with the committee," Professor Blackwell almost shouted.

I had had a difficult time locating him. I had gone to his office a few times and found it locked, even though the posted schedule on the door said that he was supposed to be available all day. I was wondering whether Professor Blackwell had stayed home ill when I saw one of his graduate students in the hall. He told me that the professor preferred using a small desk in his lab instead of the spacious office. I had to go through narrow tunnels between all sorts of equipment to reach his small office in the lab, which turned out to be a thirty square-foot area partitioned from the rest of the huge lab by six-foot high boards. There was no place for me to sit, so I stood in the gap between the boards as I talked to Professor Blackwell.

"I understand that you don't want to be on the committee," I said. "But I'm on the committee and I have to find out a few things from you."

"The whole idea of a committee is ridiculous. The facts are crystal clear. The guy couldn't take it any more and swallowed cyanide. What's the committee going to do? Prove that a secret agent from Mars killed him?"

He spoke with vehemence, or so I thought. I was unprepared for the tone of this conversation and it took me a while to find the right words to say.

"I wouldn't dare to tell you about the purpose of the committee even if I knew. I simply want to do what I was asked to do."

"And what was that?"

"I have been asked to find out whether Gregg was under any undue pressure in his academic life."

"How would I know?"

"He worked for you for about seven or eight months, didn't he?"

"No. He set my research program back by a year or two. When he left my group I was very glad; no, I was jubilant."

"Did you ask him to leave your group?"

"I was about to. He must have seen the writing on the wall."

That statement did not agree with the contents of a letter I had seen in Gregg's file. In April, three months after Gregg started research, Professor Blackwell had written a formal letter to the department recommending that Gregg's contract be extended for another year. I reminded Professor Blackwell about his letter. He wasn't pleased and waited for a while before answering in a more conciliatory tone.

"That was poor judgment on my part. During the first few months he worked for me, Gregg read every article I ever wrote - even those not related to the research project I had given him - and came frequently to discuss the contents. I thought he was building a strong background before getting into the lab. So I recommended that Gregg be given a contract for another year. I was quite unwise in doing so."

"Why did he leave your group? Particularly after you recommended him for another year's contract."

"I have no idea."

"After he left your group he started working for Professor Turner. Did Professor Turner check with you before he accepted Gregg into his group?"

"I don't remember. But Frank has a very casual attitude. He doesn't care about any standards."

I reminded Professor Blackwell that I work under Professor Turner's supervision.

"I didn't know that. What I said is nevertheless true... about grad students in his lab. Frank doesn't weed them out. Anyone can wander into his lab and start working for a degree."

"I don't think that's true," I protested.

"Over the years he has graduated more losers than anyone else in the department."

I didn't like the direction in which our conversation had veered. I had to tell myself that I wasn't there to defend Professor Turner's reputation, but only to find out whatever I could about Gregg.

"What I want to know concerns Gregg and not Professor Turner. Was Gregg under any serious pressure?"

"I haven't had anything to do with Gregg since he left my group. I can't visualize any student working for Frank Turner under any sort of pressure. I suppose it's possible that even the tiddly-winks of research Frank does could be unbearably difficult for somebody like Gregg."

Blackwell doesn't quit once he starts cutting people down, I thought. I wasn't willing to quit either, not without getting some idea of how Gregg behaved when he was working in Professor Blackwell's lab.

"How about the time he was working under your supervision?

Was he able to take various demands on him in proper stride? Or was he getting too tense to function properly?"

Professor Blackwell looked at me intently and said, "I didn't quite get your name."

"Sankar," I said.

"Sankar, I have absolutely no intention of talking about a grad student with whom I had very little to do. I don't remember what he did or didn't do in my lab. That's history and you are simply wasting my time by continuing this conversation."

That wasn't the way I had anticipated the conversation would end. As I found my way out of Professor Blackwell's lab into the corridor irritated about his attitude, a voice from behind stopped me.

"Hi! I am Laura Blackwell, Richards's wife."

I'd have guessed that she was a freshman, except for her being dressed with better decorum. Small in stature and dark haired, she wore a long skirt with floral design on a black background and a velvety black blouse.

I said that I was pleased to meet her.

"I was in the next cubicle when you were talking to Richard."

"You do research?"

"No. I don't even have a chemistry background. I am – you might say – Richard's unpaid secretary and counselor. He needs both, twenty four hours a day."

"He wasn't in a mood to talk to me.

"Richard has been grumpier than his usual. I think he's worried about tenure, though he would never admit to being worried."

"I thought it was all decided."

"Yes and no. Richard's file is sitting on the provost's desk. So far everything is positive and all it needs is the provost's signature. It's very likely he'll sign it. Otherwise he would have a lot to explain. But you can't be absolutely certain until that hurdle is cleared."

"I can see how that can be nerve-wracking for you and Dr. Blackwell."

"Let me ask you something, if you don't mind. What's this committee you mentioned about?"

I went over my befuddled understanding of the committee's mission and added, "All I'm doing is trying to get an idea of Gregg Westover's graduate studies and whether they have anything to do with his suicide."

"Gregg was in Richard's lab for nearly two semesters. Since I am a constant fixture in the lab, I talked to him several times. All I can say is that he's very sly and not altogether trustworthy. After a while you feel you want to get away from the guy as far as you can."

I wanted to find out more about Gregg from Laura Blackwell, but she was called in by the loud voice of her husband.

"There's too much jealousy in the department. I think there are some people out there who want to take Richard down a notch or two," Laura Blackwell said as she hurried back into the lab.

11:00 AM

Richard Blackwell not easy to get along. Interview went badly. Couldn't get a reading on his true feelings about Gregg leaving his lab to work with Prof. T. Laura Blackwell seems to know more about Gregg. I should talk to her again.

*   *   *

John Spikes' name was next on my list. He was the grad student who had roomed with Gregg for a while.

I saw John's silhouette against the lighted window as I walked through the smells of organic solvents. He was wearing a baseball cap, beak toward the back, and scribbling in a lab notebook. I wondered whether I could drag him out of the pungent solvent fumes before questioning him.

"I can't leave now. I have to keep checking this column every five minutes for a couple of hours."

So I had to sit in the cramped quarters and inhale a few likely carcinogens while I talked to John Spikes about Gregg.

"He was a jerk - a hundred per cent jerk."

Perhaps that was the best anybody could have said about Gregg, but I wanted some details.

"You roomed with him for a while, didn't you?"

"We shared an apartment for a semester. That was all I could take."

"When was that?"

"Last Fall."

"That was Gregg's first semester here?"

"Yes. I had a large apartment and Professor Fuller suggested that I might accommodate one of the new grad students who was coming to work with him. I agreed without checking on the guy."

"Did you say that Gregg came to work with Professor Fuller?"

"Yes."

If Gregg had come to work with Professor Fuller, why did he start working with Professor Blackwell, change his mind again and switch to Professor Turner? Why hadn't Professor Fuller mentioned his contacts with Gregg to the committee? He could at least have told me whatever he knew about Gregg. After all, I was supposed to look into Gregg's past.

I told John Spikes how I was drafted into the committee and what I had done since then. I mentioned the conversations I had had and added, "Professor Fuller talked as though he didn't know Gregg. I suppose he forgot ever meeting him."

"He was acting one hundred per cent Fuller," John said. "Let me tell you what happened."

Professor Fuller, according to John Spikes, frequently went on recruiting trips to other colleges and universities. If a student showed enthusiasm for his work, Professor Fuller would spare no effort to get him admitted to the graduate program, even if the student's past performance was very poor.

"What has Fuller got to lose? If the guy is good, Fuller gets a grateful slave in the lab. If he isn't, the grad college will throw him out in a couple of years. They aren't going to blame the faculty for anything. Anyway that's how I got here. My senior grades were bad, really bad. I was in love with a bimbo and couldn't care less for my studies. I could never have gotten into grad school with the type of grades I had in my junior and senior years. I met Fuller when he came to visit my college and told him about my troubles. You know what the cunning bastard said? He told me that he had an unusually challenging research problem that none of his grad students were willing to tackle. It was one of those problems that make you famous the moment you solve it. He was going to get me an assistantship, even if he had to fight with the president of the university. The way he talked, it sounded as though he was going to put his reputation on the line for my sake. And for my part, I was supposed to give a shot at this marvelous unsolved problem. If I didn't succeed in the first year I could switch to a safer idea and still get the degree. It all sounded great and I was so inspired about the stuff that I couldn't sleep for several days."

"How did it work out?"

"What do you mean?"

"Were you able to solve this special problem?"

"There never was such a problem. It was just the standard spiel Fuller goes through to get grad students to work for him. Except I didn't know it then. Most of us just entering grad school after a hectic B.S. program where they never give you enough time to think, wouldn't know the difference between original research and washing test tubes. It took me three years to find out that what I was doing was routine crap. The way it stands now is that, if I finish this project, I'll get a degree and then I can start hustling for work like all the other PhDs coming through the pipeline. If I don't finish the project I may never get a job since people will want to know what I've been doing for all these years in the lab."

"Sorry to hear that."

"That's it. You are told all these great things about research but ninety- nine per cent of what we do is pretty stupid. You do it just so some professor continues to get his god-damned grants."

It occurred to me that Gregg Westover had found out about Professor Fuller's recruiting style, possibly from John, and had wiggled out of the professor's grip before it was too late.

"Did you tell this to Gregg when he first came?"

"I didn't have to."

"What do you mean."

"When I came to work for Fuller I didn't know any better. It was different with Gregg. He had been in grad school for several years before he came here. He knew the Fuller types. He was using Fuller to get himself a job."

"Then why did he go to work with Blackwell?"

"Once you get the job you can work with anyone in the department. The contract doesn't say you have to work with anyone specific. Only I felt obligated to work with Fuller because I thought he gave me a chance to go to grad school. Gregg, for his part, didn't have anything you and I would call a conscience. He was totally free of such limitations. He came here and saw that Blackwell was a more desirable supervisor."

"Why did he leave Professor Blackwell's lab then?"

"I've no idea. But I'm pretty certain that Gregg saw some advantage in the move. He'd never do anything except for selfish motives."

The only reason for my being there, smelling organic solvents while talking to John, was to find out whether Gregg was reacting to academic pressure when he took the cyanide. I asked John what he thought.

"That's a stupid question. How can you tell? We are all under pressure. You don't think I'm not stressed working for Fuller?"

"What I meant was whether anything unusual happened during the last week that made Gregg kill himself?"

"I have no way of knowing."

John saw Gregg the day before the tragedy when he came to borrow a battery charger. Gregg evidently told John the same things he told Martha Gwinn, that he was planning to quit grad school and go into junior high teaching. He was optimistic. I asked John whether he knew about the termination letter and whether Gregg had received it.

"News to me. Gregg didn't say anything about that. In fact he babbled as though he was still a TA."

I wondered whether Gregg was exhibiting bravado or was truly unconcerned about continuing his university studies. I might never know.

11:45 AM

Plot thickens. Gregg came to work for Prof. Fuller. But he started research in Blackwell's group. Fuller hasn't been completely open in the comm. meeting. He must have some resentment toward G.

Spikes' description of G fits Conrad's. I am beginning to wonder why anybody should care about G's suicide. Am I missing something?

*   *   *

"I conversed with Gregg three-four times. The first time was when he came to ask me about working in my lab. That was September four - no, five - months ago. The meeting was brief. I told him that there was a desk and lab space for him, if he wanted to work in my group," Professor Turner said. We were sitting across from each other at a corner booth in the university cafeteria. Professor Turner spread his lunch - a croissant sandwich, salad, soup, apple pie and a big pot of coffee - over most of the table leaving very little space for my bean tostada and coffee cup. I had forgotten the peanut butter sandwich – the one Meera had packed the day before – on my book shelf.

"Did he tell you why he was leaving Professor Blackwell's group?" I asked.

"He tried to talk about some atrocities in Blackwell's lab, but I cut him short. I wanted to restrict the conversation to business. I saw Gregg the second time two-three weeks later, when the transfer was complete. At that time I gave Gregg a warm-up research project. Something to do with making a few compounds and building a rotating sector."

I recalled Gregg telling me about his reluctance to synthesize chemicals.

"How did he do in the lab?" I asked.

"Not well. Very badly, to be precise. The design of the sector was a complete flop. Any undergrad with two units of lab to his credit would've done better. The money spent for the machine shop was a complete waste. And he didn't make any of the compounds."

I didn't think it was necessary to mention Gregg's total lack of enthusiasm for synthesis. Instead I asked, "Did you let Gregg know that he wasn't doing well in the lab?"

"No. I thought I'd wait for a full semester before giving him an earful."

Professor Turner wore a cowboy shirt, bola tie, jeans and boots with pointed toes. His accent, however, betrayed his New England origins.

I had several questions for Professor Turner about his dealings with Gregg, but I didn't feel comfortable talking to him. I was afraid that I might offend him by not phrasing the questions appropriately. Professor Turner was my employer and, if I were to give the impression of being a hot-shot investigator looking into his relations with his grad students, I might lose my job before the next committee meeting. Fortunately, Professor Turner guessed my thoughts.

"You want to know what I know about Gregg, right?"

"Yes. It would be useful for my committee report."

"Very little. I know very little about Gregg - almost nothing."

"You didn't check his background before letting him into the lab?"

"No! Does that sound unusual to you?"

I nodded, since that was the safest thing to do.

"Well, Sankar, there are two philosophies on how to work with grad students. In one the professor is trail boss, prodding the beast to the end. That's what Blackwell does and I don't like it. Indeed I don't like the guy. In my philosophy, the professor leaves the students alone so that they could think for themselves. I neglect my students until they come crying for help. Of course, if I don't see signs of progress in a year, I tell them to get the hell out of my lab."

"I'm sure the good students appreciate that," I said quickly, glad for the opportunity to compliment.

"That philosophy is for grad students only. With post-docs I expect blood, sweat, toil and tears, besides a stream of articles."

1:30 P.M.

Clearly Gregg wasn't sitting on a hot burner. What stressed him? Must be something from outside the Chem. Dept. So there really isn't much I can do. I doubt whether I'll get any more info. even if I go on with this senseless routine.

Chapter 6

The True Purpose of the
Committee Revealed

W hen I can't see the next step, which is fairly often, I go for
a coffee break. That was what I did on that Tuesday
afternoon once I had finished talking to the last graduate student
on my list.

The written word always carries a greater weight in
academic circles than the spoken one, so my original plan was to
write a report to the committee after the interviews. I was quite
aware of the problems that beset the graduate students, having
experienced many of them personally a decade ago. Among my
own past and continuing worries were too little pay for so much
work, lack of opportunities for research into promising areas, the
pressures of time and tempo for publishing before others do while
avoiding the mistakes of hurried work, and the extremely
uncertain job market.

When Professor Fuller mentioned in the committee
meeting the possible pressures on Gregg Westover, I instantly
recalled my own experiences. I thought that the story behind
Gregg's death in the lab might show to the public the frustrations
researchers experience in the fast-paced scientific world. I was

prepared to write it down forcefully and accurately for everyone's benefit.

It became clear, however, even during the first interview with Martha Gwinn, that Gregg wasn't the type of graduate student I had visualized. He had no interest in intellectual matters and no particular ambition to achieve and hence none of the accompanying worries. What I had found out about Gregg's life in grad school was best left unwritten. Certainly it would not help me in any way, if I mentioned Gregg's blackmailing talents, Professor Fuller's half-lies in recruiting grad students, Professor Blackwell's unwillingness even to talk about his previous grad student or Professor Turner's total ignorance of Gregg's background and his let-things-evolve attitude. What could I say to the members of the committee other than that I couldn't find out why Gregg had killed himself? I was disappointed that the case gave me no opportunity to write a clever report and advance my own career. Nevertheless, I decided to write a short memo on the day's activities. Over the years I've found that's the only way to get rid of mental debris.

*   *   *

I had composed a rough draft of my report - which said in two pages that I had no idea why Gregg killed himself - and was walking toward the computer room with the intention of using one of the better printers, when I heard my name being called. It was Professor Fred Findlay. He was wearing the same clothes he had worn the day before, except they were even more crumpled.

"I'll buy you a cup of coffee, if you're ready for a break," he offered.

I wondered what he had in mind. I had already exceeded my coffee quota for the day but I went along out of curiosity.

"What did you think of the meeting yesterday?" Fred Findlay asked as we sat at a table in the non-smoking section of the cafeteria. I was searching for words when Fred answered his own question. "It was an unusual meeting, very unusual."

"Yes," I said.

"Have you done any of the things you're supposed to do?"

I was giving a report of what I had done as Fred looked vaguely to the side. "Sankar," he interrupted in the middle of a sentence, "You and I could be in a very difficult position, if we don't watch out."

"I don't understand."

"I'm sure you don't know the politics in this department, being new and all that. The real purpose of this committee, I believe, is to make Turner's life miserable and reduce his importance in the department."

"I don't understand," I repeated like an idiot.

"Frank Turner is not popular with Czerny, Fuller and the other faculty that have the real power in the department."

I recalled Professor Turner's comments on Professors Czerny and Fuller. I said, "I know that Professor Turner tends to be critical of the administration."

"That's not the issue. You can be as nasty as you want provided you haul in the research dollars. Dollars and more dollars."

"Professor Turner's research has been funded. I'm paid on his grant."

"Yes... but that isn't enough. They probably expect him to double or triple his share of research dollars."

"I think Professor Turner does good research. For a sixty year old man he is still lively, brimming with new ideas."

"Sankar, don't confuse research with research dollars. This university, like many other universities now, depends on research dollars. Every time someone gets a grant, the university gets a large percentage as overhead. They should really call it underhand. It is the overhead money that gives these asinine administrators their power. Even if you do first class research, it's no use to them unless it's funded. They will take heavily funded, third rate research any day, over first rate, unsupported research."

A feeling of intense distress came over me. Not that anything Fred said was completely new to me, but I didn't want to be reminded of the grant-greedy universities and my own precarious existence as a researcher in one of them. I was also taken by surprise at Professor Findlay's bold talk for he had appeared, during the committee meeting, as an ardent subscriber to toe-the-line philosophy, one who would agree two hundred and fifty per cent with the leader.

"I was told by one of the mealy-mouthed vice-presidents that any research that isn't funded is a hobby and they don't encourage the pursuit of hobbies on this campus," Professor Findlay added.

"So what are they going to do to Professor Turner?"

"Well, to start with, Czerny and company canceled a graduate course Frank was supposed to teach."

"I thought there wasn't sufficient enrollment."

"No. It was meant to be a punishment. You can be sure of that. Other courses with fewer students are being taught this semester. Czerny wants to restrict Frank's contacts with the grad students."

"How is he going to do that?"

"I don't know. He may try to stop grad students from working with Frank."

"He can't do that!"

"Not easily. Not under the present rules. But Czerny is cagey, and devious to boot. I believe that he'll try to evict Frank from his lab. If Frank doesn't have lab space, he wouldn't be able to supervise grad students."

My initial reaction to Fred's comment was visceral. If Professor Turner was forced out of his lab, I'd be forced out of my job. Yet I controlled my emotions enough to ask, "What does Czerny gain by that?"

"Well, that could force Frank Turner into early retirement. The administration could then hire someone with bigger research grants, someone like Blackwell."

That wasn't reassuring.

"I don't see the connection between these schemes and what we in the committee are supposed to be doing." I had difficulty saying those words for I felt very weak.

"There isn't any. Fuller and Czerny have their own side show going on. I'm sure of it, quite sure. You and I will write our reports about how the rest of the department feels about Gregg's suicide. They will take the words out of our reports, quote them out of context and twist them to suit their purpose. If you say Gregg was under pressure, they will blame Turner for it. If you say Gregg wasn't under pressure, they will blame Turner for not properly directing a good, well-adjusted graduate student. Don't you remember what Fuller said yesterday?"

"Vaguely"

"Jim Fuller said that Turner's attitude contributed more to Gregg's suicide than anything else that had happened."

I remembered words to that effect. Fred Findlay, I now realized, had tried to warn me.

"I don't see how they can put the blame for Gregg's suicide on Professor Turner."

"They don't have to. All they have to do is cast a few doubts on Turner's abilities to direct graduate students. Then with the help of the dean and some other university committee they can come up with a convoluted procedure that will restrict Frank, and perhaps some other faculty too, from having lab space. Once the space is gone Frank can't do any research. Then they can increase his teaching load until he gets sick of it and resigns. This has happened at other universities."

The scenario sketched could have been nothing more than Fred's wild imagination. But I had been meandering in the corridors of academe long enough to know that university politics transcend even the wildest imagination. A university professor's success, no, his very survival, depends on quoting and interpreting the words of others, often with surprising conclusions. Professors like Czerny and Fuller would have no trouble analyzing whatever I wrote to show that the words meant less than, more than or other than what might appear to the untrained eye.

"Listen, Sankar. I'm an untenured professor. And you're not even on tenure-track. We can't take the risk of getting involved in inter-faculty politics. I told you my suspicions only because I want to help you."

I thanked him.

"I've got to go to the Computer Center before they close for the day. One last thing, Sankar. You didn't hear any of this from me. Right?" Fred Findlay remarked as he left and I continued to sip the bitter coffee.

*   *   *

I could not quite visualize the procedure the administration would use to deprive Professor Turner of his lab space. I was also skeptical that there really was a plan to force Professor Turner into early retirement. Fred could be paranoid. After all Fred was an untenured professor and he had to be super cautious.

As I thought of what Fred had said, I realized that, even if there was only a remote chance that Professor Turner would lose his lab space, I'd be saddled with a bad conscience unless I warned him of the possibility. Professor Turner was a very likable man and I did not want to see any harm come to him. During the four weeks I had been working in Professor Turner's lab, I had come to appreciate the freedom he had given me to do research at my own pace. It was a pleasure not to have someone breathing down my neck and hurrying me while I was collecting data. I had been thinking that, if ever I was going to have a chance to establish myself as an independent researcher, Professor Turner's lab in this university would be the place for it. I could possibly publish a few articles on my own and aspire to be the principal investigator on a grant, the first step toward a tenure-track appointment.

While my current employment as a post-doc depended on Professor Turner's mercy, my chances of moving to the next level at this university depended

on all the faculty including Professors Fuller and Czerny. Whatever the odds of my getting a faculty position in the university, they would be worse with Professors Fuller and Czerny saying nay. And they were likely to block my appointment, if they saw me as an uncooperative member of the committee. The committee work, instead of advancing my career, could very well extinguish it. Not the rosy possibility I had first envisioned.

*   *   *

I rehearsed a dozen times, while sipping coffee, what I would say to Professor Turner. The object was to warn him, without being too specific, that some people in the department would like to use Gregg's suicide as a means of questioning his abilities to direct research. It would be a relaxed chit-chat with me talking casually, almost effortlessly. Just to put him on guard but not to create panic.

- *I suppose it's all wild imagination on my part, Frank. Nothing definite; nothing substantial; just speculation. Perhaps it's my attitude - the way I see the humorous side of the faculty meetings. Nevertheless I thought I should mention. You know, it does no harm to be careful in these matters. After all suicide is irrational and people trying to come to terms with it could be even more irrational... My pleasure. Don't mention it. Yes, once this beastly thing is over I'm going to lock myself in the lab and get those rate constants.*

Well, that wasn't how the conversation actually evolved.

"Sankar, I don't want you to play any god-damned games with me. What did Fuller really say? And what did Czerny say?"

"I don't remember the exact words, Professor - uh - Frank. It's the implication that bothered me. Something to the effect that your attitude might have contributed to Gregg's suicide."

"Really! And they want to abridge my academic freedom!"

I sat there wondering how I got myself into this mess.

"The bastards! I knew all along that they were eying my lab space. I need every square inch of it."

"I don't think that Professor Czerny or the committee could possibly blame you. What I have actually found out about Gregg makes it clear..."

"Sankar, I have no intention of pursuing this conversation further. If you'll excuse me, I have work to do. And I've got no stomach for silly committees and what they do or don't do."

Professor Turner stepped out of his office taking giant strides while I stayed there for a few more minutes, disconcerted and worried.

Chapter 7

Inalienable Duties

L ittle puppies should not play with tigers." I had to hear those words of wisdom from Meera.

"I wasn't playing with anyone. I was asked to be on the committee."

"Somebody tells you to put your head in a lion's mouth, and you do that?"

"The situation is quite different." I was regretting the fact that I had told Meera about my activities of the past two days.

"Why it is different?"

She did not say, Why is it different? I knew immediately that it was going to be a one-sided argument.

"Even Professor Turner thought it would be a good experience for me to be on the committee. I trust his judgment," I said.

"Turners and Burners. What do they know about you? What do they know about your family?"

"I admit, I didn't know what I was getting into." I said. There wasn't much I could do except raise the white flag.

"You must be knowing what you are getting into. You came to this country to do research only and make yourself a name. Then to find a job that pays enough for a family. You came because we do not have opportunities in India for highly educated people like you. And I came because I am your wife only."

"Meera, we went through that before. And I'm doing as much research as anyone can possibly do." I knew that Meera's real objection had very little to do with my present activities. She wouldn't have cared whether I was on a committee or not as long my job was secure. Now she was worried that I would be forced to search for another job.

"Why are they not giving you a permanent salary when you are doing so much research and rosearch?"

"Faculty jobs are hard to get."

"You know what Ramesh did. He did not get a good job after a PhD in biochemistry. They gave him a post-doc job only. With a low salary like yours only. So he became an M.B.A. Now he is given forty thousand dollars per annum."

"I am not like Ramesh. I don't like business careers."

"You don't like business careers. Ramesh is not liking the business job also. Usha is telling me that. But he is doing that because he knows what his inalienable duties are. A man's inalienable duties are to find a job with good salary so that his family is not always poor."

If there was one thing that Meera was absolutely certain about, it was the concept of inalienable duties. When I first heard her use those words I didn't know whether she was simply sloppy with the language or whether she was being profound in calling attention to the prominent words in the famous declaration, which Meera and I had read while preparing for naturalization.

As Meera would explain, every one was born to perform certain duties. Mine, as far as I could understand, was to look for the highest paying job so that we could be as far from the poverty line as possible and could afford to send Jay to a prestigious college and to an even more prestigious medical school later. Jay's duty was to study hard so that he would have nothing less than a perfect record throughout the many school and college years before he would be admitted to a medical school.

While Meera was certain about the nature of my inalienable duties, she seemed to be somewhat vague about how well I had been performing them. When we were alone she would try to persuade me, speaking in a conciliatory tone in *Telugu*, the importance of my finding a better paying, permanent job. We must invest in a house. Jay's education would suffer unless we moved from the apartment into a house and unless we settled down in one town. My continued insistence on a research career would only diminish Jay's future opportunities.

Meera expressed an entirely different view on how well I had been meeting my duties when she talked on the phone to distant relatives, about half a dozen families, scattered in the continental United States and Canada. She would claim then that by being a dedicated researcher and a man of frugal habits I had been a good model to Jay and that she preferred that to all the riches in the world or to my being stuck in a stagnant secure job.

It was in the company of close friends, however, that my performance of the inalienable duties was least appreciated. Why was I bent on pursuing a losing career while I could be steering myself into a lucrative job that would pay better for lesser work?

At that moment, when Meera was discussing the nature of my duties, we did indeed have a trusted friend, Zach Setlow, with us. He was then politely ignoring Meera's discourse while protecting his king from Jay's savage attacks. Zach, the first person we met in Gadsden, had been making our life in the new surroundings a pleasant experience. The way that meeting had taken place undoubtedly convinced Meera, and Jay too, that Zach had been chosen as our guardian angel by the mysterious forces of Providence.

*   *   *

We had been on the road for four long days when we crossed the city limit and entered Gadsden. The sign was prominent even though there were no buildings nearby. A few very tall buildings and several square miles of surrounding sprawl appeared over the distant horizon to the west of us. I was telling myself how lucky we were to cross the continent without the slightest car trouble - not even a flat tire - when the Plymouth started coughing violently. I pulled the vehicle off the road before the engine stalled and tried to convince the worried Meera that the engine had overheated and we would be on the move again once it cooled. Meera, for her part, was thoroughly perturbed and kept on suggesting that I flag down one of the speeding cars or call Zach Setlow.

Zach's sister had given Meera his name, phone number and address and had told us to call him in case we needed help. "Don't hesitate. You can depend on him, if you are in a bind," she had told Meera. This was just before we had left New Jersey, as Meera was doing her last circuit through the university community distributing clothing, Indian groceries and other items she could not cram into the overstuffed car.

I wasn't interested in calling for help then, being in a mood for a stroll. I wanted to climb the nearby peak and survey the land where we would be living for some time to come. I was also quite certain that my trusted Plymouth, which had carried us over the yawning stretches of Texas and the steep slopes of New Mexico, would start again, once the engine was allowed to cool, and get us at least as far as the nearest motel. Meera, however, was convinced that unless I acted promptly and got help, we would be stranded amongst the massive rock outcroppings, sinister cacti and shade-less alien trees with green trunks in this strange southwestern desert. As I opened the hood to let the engine cool faster and to show Meera where the hissing sound was coming from, an unexpected thing happened. One of the radiator hoses burst open spewing out a geyser of steam and hurling a metal spring up into the air. It looked as though the car was undergoing spontaneous disintegration.

"Wow!" exclaimed Jay.

I stepped back quickly before the projectile or the hot steam touched me.

"I am telling you to call Zach for help and you are not listening. You just missed a serious accident because we are all lucky. How I am going to manage, if we start in a new town with the car in the garage and you in the hospital?"

As I walked toward Reggie's Royalburgers, about half a mile from where we were stranded, in search of a phone, I debated whether I should call Zach or not. I have never been comfortable calling friends, let alone strangers, on the phone any more than I would be barging into other people's houses unannounced. But it was a Sunday afternoon and the possibility of contacting a mechanic before midnight was very remote. Besides if I didn't give Zach a buzz, I would have to explain my actions to Meera. So I dialed Zach's number while thinking of alternate plans, if he wasn't there or didn't care to help us.

Fifteen minutes later, a small white truck drove into the parking lot and a tall man with enormous feet stepped out of it.

"I bought some hoses and a couple of gallons of water. Let's go fix your buggy," he said as he extended his hand. He had a marvelous smile partly concealed by an untrimmed moustache. He spoke in a comforting voice, I thought, and I quickly forgot my previous reservations about calling strangers. Indeed after the car had been made functional and we sat at a corner table of Reggie's Royalburgers, Zach and Jay with their hamburgers, Meera and I with French fries and salads, I felt that we had known Zach Setlow for a long time.

Meeting Zach under those circumstances not only solved the problem of the overheated engine but also the one of finding a place to live in a new town. Zach was then building an energy-conserving house about twenty miles from the city center and five miles south of where we had been stranded. He had been looking for someone to rent his townhouse near the university while he stayed in a small trailer closer to his future home. We were eager to grab the townhouse even after he told us that he would have to leave many of his belongings behind for several weeks or even months. The rent he asked for was nominal.

"One other thing. The two cats have to stay until the house is complete. The coyotes will make a pretty meal out of them, if I take them with me now."

I saw from the expression on her face that Meera was about to object to sharing the rooms with cats, but before she could say anything Jay showed his enthusiasm. "Wow! I love cats! What are their names?"

"Ding and Dong"

"Ding-dong! I'll take care of them."

Meera looked helpless.

Since that day Zach had visited us frequently, getting his belongs in and out and enjoying Meera's super hot *Andhra* cooking. The benefits of friendship with Zach became tangible quickly. Through Zach I came to meet a seventy plus year old hispanic mechanic who felt the pulse of ancient Plymouths and repaired them at modest cost and, even better, gave advice at no cost. Zach introduced Jay into a very active cub scout den, which kept him busy through the long Christmas and New Year break while I was finding my way around the new lab. I cannot say that Zach's influence had always been beneficial. One of the unwise things he did was to show Meera places that sold kitchen gadgets and groceries at bargain prices. Ever since she had been buying as though she were afraid that prices would double or triple if she didn't act promptly and empty the shelves. I suppose I shouldn't blame Zach for that, since Meera would have found those shops on her own initiative or through consultation with other women from India.

*   *   *

As Meera was expressing her displeasure at my involvement in faculty politics, instead of exclusively concentrating on my inalienable duties, I wondered what were the inalienable duties for the two black cats, Ding and Dong, that

Zach had left in our care. One of them was sitting next to the sliding door with his feet tucked in and one eye half-open. The other was rubbing against my trousers, producing a loud rumbling purr.

"I lost," Zach said.

"You shouldn't have moved the black bishop to cover the king," Jay analyzed the game.

"What do you think, Zach? Don't you think Sankar should look for a better job?" Meera pleaded her case.

"First explain to me what inalienable duties are. I know what inalienable rights are. Life, liberty, pursuit of happiness and all that crap."

"Duties are just duties. You have to do them."

"I understand, Meera. Inalienable rights are things nobody can take away from you. Duties are what you impose on yourself."

"Duties are like rights. No one can change them. You can not change them."

"You are saying that I don't have a choice. "

"No. You don't have a choice. You cannot ignore your duties."

"Woof! This is heavy stuff."

"Zach, I am only saying that my husband must do his duty."

"Please spare me Meera. I don't want to be dragged into the middle of your quarrels."

"For nearly ten years he is a post doc. All his friends get permanent jobs. But we have to go from town to town because he does not want to leave research."

Zach remained silent.

"Now the professors tricked him into a committee. He is only going to make enemies. We thought before that we could settle down in Gadsden. How is he going to get a permanent job in this town now?"

"It is not as bad as that, Meera," I interjected.

She ignored me. "What would you do, if you are treated like Sankar?" Meera persisted.

"What would I do? I don't know. I left graduate school and started my own business because I couldn't stomach academic politics."

*   *   *

Conversations with Meera tend to be one-sided affairs. Depending on the topic under discussion, Meera either responds immediately, sometimes before you finish the last sentence, or acts totally deaf. But now Meera remained quiet and pensive for a few moments and I knew why.

From the time we had met Zach, Meera had been feeling very secure in his company, as though she could depend on him for protection from any disasters in what she still thought of as an alien society. Zach, for his part, never gave the slightest indication that her trust was misplaced. Yet he remained mysterious to us for he showed no inclination to talk about his past except in passing, as he did then. In the land where Meera and I grew up, anyone who had been as much a part of our lives as Zach had been, would have given us, even if we had not shown the slightest curiosity, full details of his friends, family, hopes for the future, past triumphs and tribulations. Zach, on the other hand, was intensely reluctant to talk about himself and would brush aside any questions regarding his experiences. We knew very little about him other than that he was then building a house for himself and that he was a part owner of an electronics repair shop and a construction company. Had he always been single or was he married once? Where did he grow up? What was he planning for his future? When did he drop out of grad school? What was he studying? Meera would have liked to ask such questions. But she knew that Zach would change the topic or might even tell her that it was none of her business.

"Since you are born in this country you have that freedom," Meera said, "but my husband can't do that. We don't have any money."

"Nonsense! Sankar could quit this very moment, if he doesn't like what he's doing and start up something else."

I could guess how the dialectical debate, *sans* synthesis, would proceed. He can do anything he wants. Start a business. Be a teacher or a free lance writer. Sell real estate. There are unlimited opportunities.... No. That isn't true. There is no justice. He has to compete with people who had better opportunities all along. Besides the good jobs go to people with influence...

I stepped out into the pleasant January night.

Chapter 8

Between a Rock and
a Hard Place

After seeing Jay off at the Chavez Elementary School I turned toward the university. I wasn't anxious to get to the chemistry building; I didn't know what I should do next. Pedaling at a snail pace I thought about the predicament I was in.

It was clear that I would antagonize Professor Turner, if I worked closely with the committee, whose real purpose – as Fred explained to me – was to embarrass the professor and take away his privileges. If that were to happen I would not get a decent recommendation from Professor Turner to find another job. On the other hand, if I ignored the committee work I would certainly lose the trust of Professors Fuller and Czerny who had the real power in the department. And that would close doors for me for advancement in this department. I was, as they say, between a rock and a hard place.

I suppose when you are between a rock and a hard place you look toward heaven and indulge in some wishful thinking, dream of some miracle that would change reality into illusion and illusion into reality. That might be the only reason a new idea came to me in the first place. What, a message buried in my mind seemed to flash, if Gregg had been murdered? Once conceived the idea grew quickly. As someone who connects the dots and sees an unexpected picture, I realized for the first time that the conversations I had had the previous day indicated that it was very unlikely that Gregg would have committed suicide. Murder it must have been.

Gregg had been an unethical and unpopular student who had once tried to profit by the secret art of blackmail. Over the course of such a life he had undoubtedly collected enemies, one of them perhaps even desperate enough to poison him. Gregg's body was found in the lab, and the cause of death was established to be poisoning by cyanide, a compound available in the chemistry building. It would not be impossible for someone to carry a small quantity of cyanide and, without rousing suspicion, drop it into a soft drink cup.

Gregg shared his lab with another graduate student, Kim and an undergraduate student, Rhoda. Rhoda had left to visit her parents for Christmas break and Kim had been away for the past two weeks, visiting his dying father in Korea. The only other person who would have any reason to be in that lab, Professor Turner, was camping in the mountains.

On the day he was murdered, the Saturday before the spring semester classes started, Gregg and his killer were probably among the very few in the building. The room next to the bookshelf jutting against Gregg's desk, on the south side was a common room – just a narrow tunnel – used to store file boxes. The door between the two rooms was kept unlocked for fire safety. The killer could have entered that room from the front entrance and waited, pretending to examine the files, until Gregg stepped out for a moment and then dumped the cyanide in the cup.

As I sketched the likelihood of murder, another piece of my interviews fell into place. Martha Gwinn had told me that Gregg was expecting to get enough money to put a down payment on a ranch house. There could only be two possible sources for Gregg's sudden riches. Either he had received an inheritance - in which case he would have told Martha and celebrated openly - or he had almost succeeded in blackmailing someone. After all Gregg did have a history of blackmailing and history is apt to repeat. The person who had been the object of blackmail certainly would have a reason – a motive – to get rid of Gregg.

He or she would have the opportunity to do that. The building was usually deserted on Saturday evenings and on that day, during the last weekend before spring semester classes started, anyone could have walked into the building without fear of being noticed. Thus the two of them, Gregg and the murderer, could have agreed to conduct their business without another soul watching. Did the other person offer Gregg a soft drink doctored with cyanide? If so, did Gregg accept it without suspicion? That could be the case, if Gregg knew the other person and underestimated his or her deviousness.

The murder hypothesis raised several questions regarding who and how. But it did not raise the apparently illogical question the suicide hypothesis brought up, namely, why would Gregg commit suicide when he had been looking forward to a better life? Besides, he was the type that continues to survive by transferring their troubles to others.

What I lacked were the facts. And I had neither the skills nor the authority to collect them. A prudent course of action would be to get back to my research and stop thinking of Gregg until the next committee meeting on Monday. But that was not what I did.

As I was locking my bike to a rack next to the entrance of the chemistry building, I noticed Cathy Quintaro walking toward the building. Since she wasn't one of the faculty I felt no hesitation trying out my theory on her.

"Why is everyone so sure that Gregg committed suicide? Couldn't it have been a murder?"

"I suppose it's possible .... If you want to talk to me you have to walk to the office with me. I got to open up shop right away."

Cathy Quintaro was a petite woman, with blond hair and light blue eyes, not what I expected to see in a Latina. As she opened the office door the phone rang and for the next couple of minutes I heard her repeatedly say "yes" while she scribbled on a pad.

"That was Dr. Czerny," she said, "with a list of things I must do before he arrives at 'leven. I tell you, Dr. Sankar, this place is a mad house. I came here about a month ago...."

"About the same time I did."

"Yes. I've seen much more action in one month than during the entire three years I was in the department of Hispanic Studies .... We were supposed to have quiet time between the semesters! Let me put the machine on call-forward. I need a couple of minutes of peace before I start the day. Meanwhile someone else can put up with the calls."

"What were you doing in Hispanic Studies?"

"To begin with, I was a grad student. Then I met my husband who was and continues to be a grad student in Chicano Lit. Carlos is from Mexico but became a citizen before we met. Soon after we were married it became obvious that we couldn't afford even frijoles unless one of us got a better salary than the grad students in Hispanic Studies. Carlos was willing, actually anxious, to see me through grad school, but I wasn't that interested - not then anyway. So I started at Secretary-I level in Hispanic Studies and moved up the ladder to this job."

"I was thinking that you didn't look like someone with latin roots."

"You're right. I'm from Michigan. Used to be Cathy Van Ness.... You were saying something about Gregg."

"Did the police report say that it was suicide?"

"The police said nothing. They are still investigating. It's Dr. Czerny who's convinced that it was suicide. I heard him talk to the police sergeant. Evidently Dr. Czerny has been trying to make this into a research-one department, the best in the world. The old, unproductive faculty and their mediocre students aren't going to make the cut and some of them may find the pressure too much to bear."

I wondered whether Professor Czerny considered Gregg's supposed suicide as proof that the department, under his leadership, had entered a new era of highly competitive research.

"Why did he appoint a committee, if he was sure he knew why Gregg killed himself?"

"I have no idea, but Dr. Fuller was somehow involved in it."

"As I see it now, the committee has no real purpose." Other than causing some trouble to Professor Turner, I thought, but didn't say.

"Yes and no. It can't do anything that Dr. Czerny doesn't want it to do. But he can claim that he appointed the committee to address the issues, if something unexpected turns up. He has nothing to lose and he's protected from possible criticism."

I suppose I should have been mad at Professors Czerny and Fuller for getting me into this mess. Instead I was wonder struck at their genius for politics.

"Why did Dr. Czerny put me on the committee?"

"It was Professor Fuller's idea. He thought they should have someone from Professor Turner's group."

Since the committee had no real power and no definite goals, it didn't matter who was on it. Professors Fuller and Czerny chose the only post-doc in Professor Turner's group, me, because it would give the impression of fairness and objectivity. If anyone was duped by this charade, it was me, believing that I had a useful and rewarding task and that doing it would advance my career.

"I feel that homicide shouldn't be ruled out at this point. Do you know whether Gregg had any bitter enemies – inside or outside the department?"

"Nope. I haven't even met the guy."

"Did Czerny or Fuller say anything about where the cyanide might have come from?"

"Not to me. But I overheard Dr. Czerny saying that it came from stock."

"You mean the stockroom?"

"I think that's what he said. Yes, stockroom on the fourth floor."

"Do you know how much was used and what happened to the rest of the stuff in the bottle?"

"Nope. I'm just a grunt here."

*   *   *

It was just past eight-thirty when I left Cathy Quintaro, with the depressing feeling that I too was a grunt. I wanted to take the rest of the morning off, go bicycling to the nearby park, read a few poems that I had collected into a notebook over the years and write in my journal – the things I do when I feel the world around me confusing and distressing. I also wanted to think about a good excuse for quitting the committee. After all nothing beneficial for me was likely to come out of it, if I continued with the investigation. I could tell Professors Czerny and Fuller that my research was suffering and unless I worked overtime on the project I might be scooped by a Japanese group – a believable lie.

I would have headed for the park with my two-day-old peanut butter sandwich had I not noticed a large document, nearly twenty-five pages thick, that was undoubtedly dropped on my desk while I was talking to Cathy. It was a copy of a memo from Professor Turner to the members of the ad hoc committee. My first instinct was to ignore it, get my helmet and ankle clips, and be on my way. However, I knew that I would be thinking about the document when I should be relaxing in the park and so I turned the pages cautiously.

As I glanced through the pages of the memo, the strange world of academic politics became even stranger. Much of the document consisted of tables comparing the teaching, research and other contributions (strange word, I thought) of the various faculty members and the resources given to them by the administration. Professor Turner, according to the memo, had just one hundred square feet of lab space for each researcher working with him while Professor Czerny had five hundred square feet per researcher. Professor Turner published one and half times more research articles than Professor Fuller for every fifty thousand dollars of research funds. Professor Turner had taught, over the past three years, more students per every thousand dollars of salary than the three highest paid faculty in the department put together. During the previous six months his research articles were cited more often than those of Professor Czerny, that is if one did not count the author citing his own articles. Every table was followed by an extensive set of footnotes that explained how the data were obtained.

I was fascinated by the tables and footnotes and would have continued to examine them had I not seen the strong and provocative language of the last page. Professor Turner had thrown down the gauntlet.

"It is clear from the forgoing analysis," Professor Turner's memo stated, "that the present head of the department has been trying to abridge my academic freedom while, at the same time, ignoring the accepted procedures for dealing with academic personnel. The most recent example of his dictatorial behavior is the termination of the employment of a very promising graduate student, Gregg Westover, without consulting me, the research director, or any other faculty member familiar with Gregg's research. Gregg was a slow starter and he was not fortunate enough to have proper guidance during his first year at the University of Gadsden or during the previous years at Guadalupe University. However, during a single semester in my laboratory, he showed remarkable experimental and theoretical skills. I have no doubt that Gregg would have developed, in due course, into a first rate researcher, one we could all be proud of. Gregg would not have committed suicide, if his employment had not been terminated without due process by Professor Czerny. Clearly the head of the department is culpable. If the committee does not consider this important issue during its next meeting, I will be forced to bring it to the attention of the University Standing Committee on Academic Freedom and the President's Council on Academic Integrity. I will be glad to furnish all relevant information to the committee through my post-doctoral colleague, Dr. Sankar."

No doubt about it, I was between a rock and a hard place.

*   *   *

"The professors like Gregg's death to be a suicide so that they can blame each other. You want it to be a homicide so that you don't have to take sides. Is that it?" Zach Setlow commented when I told him that the committee had become an arena for faculty politics. We were sitting at a table near a window in the university cafeteria, Zach with his brunch of eggs, ham and hash brown potatoes and I with a cup of coffee, since it was between breakfast and lunch for me. Zach had come to the university to consult a friend in the Landscape Architecture Department and had stopped to - in his words - check on me.

"That's not quite it."

"That's the impression you gave me."

"True, I don't want to get into the middle of fights between profs. But I also feel that whatever I gathered about Gregg supports the homicide hypothesis."

"Then tell them."

"It's not as simple as that."

"Why not?"

"I don't have any facts to support the theory."

"They don't have any facts either."

That was certainly true; but that wouldn't help me.

"I know," Zach said, "the profs made up the rules of the game and you have to play according to their rules."

"That's about it."

"What happens if you refuse to play by their rules? They are not going to kill you. There is a limit to their powers."

"Perhaps nothing will happen. More likely I'll have a hard time getting a faculty position here. One no is all takes to knock me out of the race."

"In that case you'll have a better chance winning a lottery than getting into the faculty club here."

Unfortunately Zach was right, even though I was having difficulty admitting it. Even if everyone in chemistry department sings my praise, my application will never go past the dean's office. If Blackwell, with all the money and publications, was having some difficulty getting Provost's OK for tenure, what chance do I have to get a faculty appointment, let alone tenure at a later date? The only way I could even enter the race was by having connections to big guys in research and securing large grants, neither of which were within my grasp then.

"It's just that we have been moving too much. It's time to settle down and I can't think of a better place to live than this town," I said.

Perhaps because most people in this state were from somewhere else, Meera and I felt very much at home in our new surroundings, in spite of my recent worries in the department. And the warm climate is a definite plus for people who grew up on the edge of the Deccan.

"You don't have to be employed by this diploma mill to live in the state," was Zach's comment.

"Except I don't know what else I can do."

"Nonsense"

"I can't change easily, Zach."

"That's what you keep telling yourself."

"What other opportunities are there for someone like me in Gadsden?"

"Several, if you look around. You could be in real estate. It's a booming business. If Meera ever gets her computer skills up she could be a loan officer in a bank. And between the two of you, you could haul in a lot of cash."

I admired his enthusiasm, as Zach went on to list various other career-building possibilities, but felt remote from the world he was portraying. However, as I walked back to the chemistry building my thoughts took a hundred and eighty degree turn.

I have been hoping for a permanent academic career since I assume that it would amalgamate what I like to do with what I needed to do to earn a living. What if I couldn't combine the two? By trying to force a marriage between the two was I not failing in both?

I wrote into my notebook when I got into my office:

Don't antagonize Professors Fuller, Czerny or Turner; but don't worry about what they think. Get answers to your own questions and not theirs.

The stockroom from where we get most of the commonly used laboratory and office supplies was at the south end of the fourth floor. It was the last room on the right before the stairwell. The door for the narrow room where old data files were stored was right across the corridor from the stockroom entrance. I had lodged my data from pre-Gadsden years, notebook and charts for 1983 to end of 1992, in that room soon after we arrived in Gadsden; there was no space in my lab/office to accommodate them. Since the data room had to be open to every researcher in the department, the keys for it were widely distributed. The fire-safety rules required that the door between that room and Professor Turner's main lab be kept unlocked all the time. Gregg's desk was a few steps from that door and it would have been easy for someone to wait in the data room, pretending to examine files, and step into the lab to drop crystals of cyanide into Gregg's soft drink cup when he stepped out briefly.

This possibility raised two questions: how did he or she get the cyanide? When was that done? The answer to the second question was straight forward. The poison could have been secured only on that fateful Saturday. There would have been constant activity in the stockroom during the previous day, with people coming and going, and the staff watching every transaction – too much activity for anyone to steal a bottle of cyanide.

Keys for the stockroom were restricted to only a few employees, but unauthorized copies were undoubtedly floating around. If Gregg had indeed committed suicide, he must have had one of those keys. I went in to the lab to rummage through Gregg's desk. The lab was deserted since Kim was still in Korea and Rhoda was running around campus registering late for her classes. I found four university keys on a ring in Gregg's desk. One was for the entrance and another for the laboratory. I had no idea what the other two were for.

I took the keys and was trying to see whether any of them fit the stockroom lock when Morris Hayakawa asked, "What are you trying to do?"

"These are Gregg's keys. Just checking whether he could have slipped into the stockroom when no one was looking."

Morris examined the keys and said, "The two extra keys are for Professor Blackwell's labs."

"That means Gregg had no access to the stockroom."

"I can't be sure. If he had a key to the stockroom, he wouldn't carry it with regular keys."

That possibility bothered me but I didn't want to dwell on it at that moment as Morris led me to the shelf with chemicals. There was just one unopened bottle of potassium cyanide, with a plastic seal around the top, on the shelf. I assumed that they had just two bottles in stock and the missing one contained the sample that killed Gregg.

"What happened to the other bottle?"

"The police took it. I came here early on Sunday morning after Professor Czerny called and asked me to cooperate with the police. He is the one who told the police to look for cyanide bottles here."

"So the bottle was on the shelf until the police showed up."

"Yes."

"Strage, very strange."

"Why do you say that?'

"Why would anyone put the bottle back? After all the trouble sneaking into the stockroom, why come back again?"

"Maybe the bottle was never removed from here. Maybe the guy dumped some in his cup from the bottle and left."

"In that case the broken plastic seal should be near the bottle or in the trash can next to the door."

"I don't remember seeing it on the shelf. It wasn't in the trash can either. There was nothing in the trash can. I'd have noticed a plastic thingy as I was dumping my coffee cup."

"What did the police say?"

"They said nothing. Went around doing their stuff and gave me a paper before they left."

Morris showed me the receipt for items taken by the police. When I glanced at it something looked odd, though I couldn't quite put my finger on it.

"Just two bottles in stock – is that it?" I asked

"Yes."

"Would you know when cyanide was last ordered?"

"I had to find that out for Professor Czerny. We received two 250 gram bottles of potassium cyanide from KR distributors three months back on October 3, 1993. They were ordered because Professor Norton wanted to develop an experiment for seniors. He never got around to that experiment and so the bottles were sitting here for the last three months."

"You sure both bottles came from KR distributors."

"Yes. I had to look it up for Professor Czerny. It took me a while to find that order and the delivery slip."

Then I knew what was odd and puzzling me.

Chapter 9

The Cyanide Bottle Exchange

I saw Professor Niles Baxter, with a textbook and a ring-binder, entering his office. His clothes and hands were covered with bands of chalk dust. Undoubtedly he was returning from a lecture.

"Yes," he said, when I asked whether he could spare a few minutes for me, "but first I must wash this damned chalk dust off my hands and relieve myself of what I couldn't dump on the students. Have a seat while you wait"

I wondered whether there was a disease called chalkosis of the lungs and whether epidemiological research one day would show the prevalence of it among the teaching faculty. If any group wanted to do research on this subject, it should start with Professor Baxter. I could easily see him pacing back and forth in front of the black board, brushing his jacket and slacks against the chalk tray, scribbling ferociously and thumping the board with the eraser while the white dust rose, covering his clothes and the table in front of him.

I had been to the stockroom looking for the cyanide bottle. What I had found was quite unexpected. It had taken me a while to realize it and then my heart started racing. I thought that

I had, in front of me, the key to Gregg's murder, though the procedure necessary to find the actual killer remained unclear at that moment. I had thought of calling Zach Setlow to discuss my findings, but I didn't want to explain why I was still going ahead with the investigation after complaining about my predicament.

I didn't think it would be wise to talk to the senior faculty, Professors Fuller, Czerny or Turner. I knew I couldn't defend my sketchy theory in their august and intimidating presence. Fred Findlay, on the other hand, would be an ideal person to talk to about this matter. He had been open with me and I had felt very comfortable talking to him on the previous day. So I went to find Fred but he had already left the department, leaving a note to the effect that he wasn't feeling well.

Niles Baxter, five years younger than me, was probably the lowest ranking faculty member in the department. Even though he was quarrelsome during the committee meeting, I thought he might give me a sympathetic ear and perhaps even help me with the investigation. At any rate I was certain that I'd be able to have a relaxed conversation with him about my recent discovery.

Whatever Niles was doing, it took him a long time. His room, I couldn't help noticing, was one of the most untidy places I had ever seen. The window was blocked by wooden crates containing books and papers, leaving only a thin slit. The light coming through it made the already dim room appear hazy.

"Damn students! You can't even sit on the throne without someone asking you about your grading policy," Niles said as he came in. He removed his tie and tossed it toward the crates.

I wanted to bring up the topic of conversation gradually for I needed his cooperation. I said, "You mind if I call you Niles?"

"Not in the least! By the way did you see that memo your boss wrote?"

I didn't want to talk about it. "Yes, but I didn't read it," I lied.

"Read it! Real juicy stuff. I tell you we're going to have fist fights around here... Fuller was raging mad. I saw him this morning. He gave me an earful about how Turner had been ruining the graduate programs and the reputation of the department. He wants to devote the next meeting entirely to cussing and discussing Turner's memo."

I was reminded: That would be a no-win but a sure-fail situation for me. Whichever side I chose, or even if I didn't choose a side, I was likely to antagonize the faculty. But I didn't want to think about my relation with the faculty. I said hurriedly, "Niles, I wanted to tell you that Gregg didn't kill himself."

"Really?"

"Yes. He was murdered. I think I may be able get some leads on the killer."

"Well, that'll stir things up in this place. How did you come up with this idea?"

"I can explain my ideas better, if we go to the stockroom."

*   *   *

As we walked to the stockroom, I explained the layout of Gregg's lab and how easy it would have been for the killer to stay in the adjacent room used for data storage until the opportune moment. I was pleased that Niles showed interest in my theory.

Once in the stockroom I showed him the lone potassium chloride bottle on the shelf and the police receipt.

"The bottle up there came from KR supplies. The open bottle taken by the police came from BN supplies."

"So?"

"According to the stockroom records both bottles should be from KR supplies."

"I'm not sure what you are driving at, Sankar."

"It means that the bottle from which the cyanide came is not the stockroom bottle."

"So how did it end up here?"

"Simplest explanation is that who ever poisoned Gregg exchanged the stockroom bottle with the one from his or her lab."

"Why do that?"

"I can only guess. Suppose only after poisoning Gregg, the killer realized that putting the opened bottle back in his or her lab would make it conspicuous. Other workers in the lab might notice it and report. By exchanging the two bottles you are directing the attention away from your lab."

Niles seemed lost in thought. After a while he said, "Are you coming up with this scenario because you want to support you murder hypothesis?"

"No, but look at the facts. Assuming it was suicide, why would Gregg take the trouble of exchanging bottles? "

"There is one serious flaw in your theory, Sankar."

"What is that?"

"Why would any lab have its own supply of cyanide when it is readily available in the stockroom? It would be like buying paper and pencils from Office Depot when you can readily check them out from the stockroom."

I was surprised that Niles raised that question until I realized that even though he was a faculty member, he had far less experience than I had in research and grants.

"What will you do, Niles, if you have money left in a grant and the deadline for spending it is fast approaching?"

"I haven't gotten that far yet."

"Well, instead of letting the money go back to Uncle Sam, you will order chemicals and lab supplies for future use. After all you don't get anything free from the stockroom. So why not buy your own stuff when you can?"

"Makes sense."

"Find any more objections to my theory of murder?"

"No! I think it's brilliant. Here is what I understand. Suppose you are the killer. No.. no. Let's make Fuller the killer. That even rhymes. He takes the cyanide sample from an unopened bottle in his lab and dumps into the cup. Only after doing the damage he realizes that if he were to put the bottle back someone in the lab would notice it and report to the police. So he trades it with the bottle in the stockroom to divert attention. That's the idea, right?"

"Yes, that's it."

"Now how are you going to find out the criminal?"

Thinking about this conversation later, I wished Niles had not brought up that question. Until that moment I was thinking that I'd report my findings to the police, without worrying about Fuller's committee, and get back to my lab bench. But once Niles put that question to me I couldn't stop thinking of how I would proceed from that point. And once I start thinking about a problem, I become obsessed with it and I can't forget it. It didn't take long for me to come up with a plan.

"I think we can zero-in on the lab from which the cyanide came. We can even do that without anyone knowing that we are investigating the murder," I said. I used the word *we* deliberately. I wanted Niles' help because I knew that proceeding alone with the investigation from now on would be impractical and possibly risky.

"How are you going to do that?"

"The bottle in question was ordered from BN distributors by some researcher. If we look at the purchase orders for the last few months, we can find out who that was."

I was aware that would narrow the search to a particular lab in the building but would leave the question of who in that lab unanswered. One thing at a time, I told myself and shuffled that worry out of my head.

"You think through everything, don't you?" Niles said. "You really are a sleuth, Sankar."

It was time to divulge the plan. I said, "I need your help."

"For what?"

"Financial Affairs across the street won't let me look into the purchase orders. I found that out the very first day on the job."

"Why not?"

"I'm not a faculty member. At least that's what the woman in the office told me."

"That's ridiculous. Let's go take care of it."

It didn't turn out to be that simple. The woman I'd faced weeks before - she with stern expression and fluffy hair that occupied thrice the volume of her head - met us at the door, essentially blocking us from entering the room. She wore very tight pants that hugged her legs, the type exercise enthusiasts use, and a very loose blouse. The combination made her look like a gaudy flower pot supported on a pair of thin dowels.

"Did you want to see the orders on your grants?" She asked Niles.

"I want to see all the orders for the last few months."

"I can't let you do that unless the head of your department authorizes it."

Niles mumbled a few obscenities as the woman closed the door gently but firmly.

We walked away from the business office as Niles described in detail all the bureaucratic nightmares that resulted from the new management style. I was still absorbed in my own schemes and couldn't pay attention to Niles. I suggested, "Let's get Professor Czerny's permission."

"No way! I'm not going to face that bastard unless I've got to."

My heart sank. Alone I'd have no luck in explaining to Professor Czerny the reason for examining the purchase orders. He might not even agree to see me. Or he might agree to see me after Easter. I didn't think that I could go ahead without a faculty member providing at least tacit support for my cause while I was pleading with Professor Czerny.

"We can make it a short visit," I ventured, "I'll do most of the talking."

"Nope. My chances of getting tenure here are infinitesimally small. But if I punch that guy in the front office, which I'm likely to do if he says no, I'll never be employed again

- not even by the branch campus of Podunk Community College."

Chapter 10

Disappointing Results

When I get a promising idea in research, I can hardly sit down or stay alone. I get the feeling that unless I talk to someone I might not be able to contain myself. Yet I also feel a certain hesitation - even fear - of saying anything to anyone. I am worried about finding out that my idea is worthless, or I have ignored an important step in logic or, worse yet, it has already been suggested by someone better and brighter than me. I had those feelings of exhilaration, on the one hand, and fear of ridicule, on the other hand, when I noticed the cyanide bottles were switched. When Niles Baxter refused to go with me to see Professor Czerny, the exhilaration went down and the fear of ridicule went up.

I was afraid of seeing Professor Czerny for other reasons as well. I was certain that he had received Professor Turner's memo and had probably figured out my role in warning Professor Turner. How was he going to express his displeasure at my doings?

As I paced the corridors I realized that I would not be able to drop the case. My worries would only increase if I kept on thinking about what Professor Czerny might say. It would be far less stressful to tell him the hypothesis, even if it led to patronizing ridicule, than to keep it to myself. So I gathered all my courage and walked to Professor Czerny's office.

When I asked to see Professor Czerny, Cathy Qunitaro said: "I don't think he will see anyone now, particularly you. He's pretty upset about the memo your boss sent. He says it's a bunch of lies and he'd have Turner fired except for the tenure rules."

"Would you check with him any way. It's rather important."

"I'll ask him. But I'm sure the answer is going to be no. He has to leave soon for an important luncheon date with the President." Cathy knocked on the closed door and walked in.

I was expecting to see Cathy come out with her head shaking horizontally, that being the sign for a no in this culture. To my surprise, it was Professor Czerny who came out with a broad smile and an extended hand. "Sankar, I don't have much time, but I'm sure we can visit for a short while... Cathy, call the President's secretary and let her know that I'll be a bit late." He showed me into his office while Cathy looked at me with a smile and squinted.

"Sankar, I want to tell you how pleased I am at the excellent work you've been doing for the committee."

"Thanks," I said bewildered.

"I'm sure you've seen the memo your boss wrote. I am afraid Frank has been overly imaginative. I know that he doesn't like my administrative style. I admire his independent style. But no one in his right mind could deny that I have brought distinction to this department."

I realized that I was being drawn more deeply into the faculty politics and my uneasiness grew.

"When you try to improve the research productivity of a department you are likely to rattle a few cages," Professor Czerny continued. "Frank has no reason to complain about the support this department has been giving him. He should actually expect a reduction in the departmental support unless his research productivity goes up both in quality and quantity."

I felt like begging, please leave this poor, poor post-doc out of your battles, but I couldn't say anything.

"I asked Jim Fuller to devote the next committee meeting to a discussion of Frank's memo. I am writing my own memo to the committee which contains significant information Frank conveniently forgot to include. I'd understand if you don't want to be too involved in these matters. But I want you to consider all the facts as objectively as you can and give your input to Jim. I have always valued my co-workers opinions."

I uttered a weak yes, not knowing what else to say.

"I'm sure you didn't come to discuss this silly temper tantrum of your boss. So what brings you here?"

"I came to talk about the committee work," I said as I collected my thoughts.

It would take me a very long time to explain my activities since the time I first met Professor Czerny on Monday morning. And if Professor Czerny were to cross-examine my deductive reasoning, I could very well make a fool of myself. I thought it would be better if I made my request brief, with as few words as possible.

"Since I haven't digested Professor Turner's memo and haven't seen yours, I will wait. Meanwhile I have a request."

"Digested! I like that word, Sankar. Very appropriate. What's your request?"

"I'd like to examine all the purchase orders for chemicals during the last few months."

"Why?"

I'd already decided not to go too far into explanations. However, I didn't want to tell a lie. I said, "I believe that I will find some information relevant to Gregg."

"I'm afraid I don't see the connection. Unfortunately we don't have enough time to go over the details, but I trust your reasoning, Sankar."

Oh! What a beautiful day!

"The Financial Affairs personnel are the grouchiest around here. I can't blame them. They take so much flak from the faculty, usually without rhyme or reason. So they aren't going to roll out the red carpet for you, even after I give the OK. So let's do it differently. I will ask Cathy to help you. She'll stay with you while you are going through the files and make sure that you are given all the information you need."

Green light after green light! Soon I will be out of the smog-drenched traffic and into the beautiful mountains and majestic canyons!

*   *   *

Waiting is worrying. It has always been like that for me. I waited two hours for Cathy. While she finished whatever she had been doing and then kept her luncheon date with her husband, I worried all the time about the different ways my plan could go wrong. I was convinced, more than ever, that Gregg was indeed murdered. However, as I waited and worried my hope of discovering the killer dwindled at an exponential rate, as they say in my trade.

I knew how purchase orders were processed, having submitted a few immediately after I joined the department and having had to go through the bureaucratic mazes. Every time someone in the department needed a chemical, a piece of equipment or a particular service, he filled out an order blank and indicated the grant number to which the cost was supposed to be charged. The order was typed by someone in Financial Affairs who, after making sure that the researcher was authorized to use the money on that particular grant, submitted it to the head of the department. After a day or two, the head's signature appeared on the form and then it was sent to the University Grants Office. The head, Professor D. M. Czerny, had a characteristic signature. The three initials of his name were like the bold, ragged peaks of the nearby San Miguel range, while the rest of the letters merged into one long line, drooping toward the horizontal like the *bajada* from those majestic peaks.

At the University Grants Office busy accountants researched to make sure that there was enough money in that particular fund. When the grant was first awarded, the budget stipulated how much could be spent on each category, such as chemicals, travel, supplies, computer charges and equipment. The accountants also examined these restrictions. There must be enough money in the specified category before the order could be approved. Excess funds from one category could not be transferred to another category except by permission from the more sagacious accountants at the headquarters of the granting agency.

Once the order form met the accountants' tests, it traveled to the office of the Dean of Physical and Mathematical Sciences. The dean was an ex-mathematician with a reputation for poor teaching. He rarely looked at these forms. Perhaps in some critical cases he might scrutinize the order forms to see that the items ordered were essential for research (he admired research without any equipment) but for the most part he left the duties of signing the forms to the Assistant to the Dean, who was not the same person as any of the many Assistant Deans. After a proper amount of waiting at the dean's office the order form went to the Office of the Vice President for Research whose purpose it was to ascertain that the purchase of any of the items on the order form would not be a violation of the university policies for research or any of the state and federal laws that govern research. The vice president was a busy man, surprisingly young - barely past thirty - to occupy such an exalted position. He looked at each form himself, rather than delegating authority to a less talented assistant. Because of the vice- president's extreme devotion, the order form stayed for several days on his mammoth desk before it was approved.

From the vice president's office the form traveled two long miles to a warehouse, the seat of the university purchasing "Czar," the Director of Physical Resources and the Vice-

President for Planning. It was the duty of the Czar to make sure that the tax payers' money was spent wisely. If he was unconvinced that the university was getting the lowest price for the items about to be purchased, he would call for bids even if the researcher who had instigated these proceedings, some three weeks back, had already checked the prices.

The order form became the official purchasing order when the czar decided to sign it. Then a copy of the form - the yellow copy - was sent to the Financial Affairs office which, without sorting or indexing, put it in a hard-to-open binder with metal straps.

I would be looking through these binders. A researcher, I estimated, submitted five orders per month on the average. There were at least a hundred researchers in the department, counting grad students, post-docs like myself and the faculty. Thus I'd have to scan about a thousand yellow copies if I wanted to find out the names of the people who had ordered cyanide during the last two months. It became painfully obvious to me that I could easily miss a form or overlook an entry unless I searched very carefully.

It occurred to me then, that even if I managed to scrutinize each yellow copy, I could fail to find some of the recent orders due to an occasionally used shortcut to the lengthy procedure of sending the order through inter-departmental mail. The short cut, discovered by an enterprising graduate student in a hurry to get his PhD., was called walking-the-order-through. When a researcher wanted something badly and couldn't wait the usual three weeks it took for the order to drift to the czar and another week for the vender to respond, he would use the walk-through technique. He would collect a dozen other grad students - some of them pretty disreputable in their looks - and all of them would march like a phalanx, carrying the order form, to the office where a signature was to be procured. The sight of so many students usually intimidated the secretary at the desk and she grabbed the order form, without anyone so much as requesting her to do so, ran into the room where bold signatures were produced by anonymous hands and returned, with the signed order, all in no time. Thus an order was sometimes walked through from the chemistry building to the purchasing office in about an hour. The Czar did not like this; he probably felt like a general surrendering territories when he agreed to process these forms. He got his revenge after the mob left. Instead of mailing those orders, he phoned them and billed the charges for the phone call and related expenses to the grant. Thus an enthusiastic researcher who had walked his order for a five dollar chemical might find that the actual cost came to twenty dollars. The Czar kept the yellow slips on his desk until he could ascertain the phone charges and the handling expenses for the rush orders. Hence the yellow slips came back to the Financial Affairs office weeks after the purchased item was received. If the cyanide order had been walked-through recently, the only records on it might still be with the Czar.

*   *   *

I tried to keep my anxieties down as we searched through the yellow copies of the purchase orders. It was past four by the time Cathy and I finished the search and found only a single order for a bottle of potassium cyanide from BN distributors, on a grant administered by Professor Richard Blackwell. As we came to the end of the files, I realized that I could have done the whole thing in a shorter period without Cathy. She was completely unfamiliar with the chemical nomenclature and would stop to read out the name of every chemical that sounded similar to potassium cyanide. She was also curious about what the researchers did with various supplies and kept on interrupting me.

"So what does it all prove?" Cathy asked as we were leaving the Financial Affairs office.

"Nothing definite. It suggests, though, that the cyanide that killed Gregg came from Professor Blackwell's lab and one of the persons working in that lab probably killed Gregg."

I explained my theory about the cyanide bottles to Cathy. Perhaps I shouldn't have done that. Even a tyro of a detective would have been more circumspect than I had been

*   *   *

The best time to search a lab was between five-thirty - by which time the last lingering secretary left - and seven, when the evening students and nocturnal researchers started trickling into the building. I waited for the opportune time sipping coffee in front of a window on the second floor of the cafeteria and watching the chemistry building, right across the mall.

Even though we had searched through the purchase orders without any particular bias, it occurred to me, when we finally found it, that I should have been paying special attention to the orders from Professor Blackwell's research group. Gregg had been with that group of ten to fifteen researchers - Professor B was very well funded - for nearly a year. It wasn't inconceivable that, with his record of black-mailing and probably other unsavory activities, Gregg might have pushed one or more of them into an inescapable corner. Neither John Spikes nor Professor Blackwell had mentioned any such activities on Gregg's part nor did I particularly inquire about them. It was, of course, possible that neither of them knew of any shady activity.

I was admiring the rather abrupt change in color - the tall windows of the chemistry building now reflected the orange-red sunset - when I noticed Professors Fuller and Czerny and Cathy Quintaro emerge from the building.

They stood in front, talking for a few minutes, before going their separate ways - Professor Czerny to his Mercedes parked south of the building, Professor Fuller bicycling north and Cathy going around the building presumably to meet her husband in the Department of Hispanic studies. A few minutes later Richard and Laura Blackwell came out of the building in a hurry and walked briskly to the parking lot. It was safe for me to go and do the sleuthing in Professor Blackwell's lab. I had Gregg's keys to that lab in my pocket.

My search through Professor Blackwell's lab went slowly, while I was feeling the anxiety that one of the researchers would wander in and report my unauthorized presence. All the chemicals were arranged in alphabetical order on the shelves next to the west wall of the nearly two thousand square-foot laboratory. I could not find a potassium cyanide bottle anywhere on that shelf. That would have been distressing enough. To add to my frustration there was a gap and a ring mark on the thin layer of dust where I had expected to find the bottle, indicating that the bottle had been removed recently. I searched on the laboratory benches hoping that someone forgot to shelve the bottle but couldn't find the missing bottle.

In the end I had to accept reluctantly that I could go no further with the case on my own. If I wanted the mystery solved, I should report my findings to the police, directly or through Professor Fuller, and let them handle it from there. Their crime lab techs undoubtedly had the tools to investigate systematically. The police could also question under oath - which I couldn't do - each and every researcher in Professor Blackwell's group. The thought of reporting my findings to the police did not make me feel any better. In the first place I wanted to get the credit for the investigation. In the second place, the police might not take my hypothesis seriously and I might be ignored, particularly if they stopped to talk to Professors Fuller or Czerney.

It was with gloom then that I left Professor Blackwell's lab. As I was leaving I felt a strange fear, as if the killer were right behind me, watching every one of my movements. I hurried out of the hostile territory with my heart beating loudly.

*   *   *

After leaving Professor Blackwell's lab, with a sense of utter failure, I had sat at my desk behind the vacuum rack, going over the events of the past three days. There was only one possible explanation for the missing bottle: someone in that lab got wind of my activities and removed it before I could prove that it had come from the stockroom. I saw no way I could progress beyond this point. I had no authority to question anyone in that laboratory.

I felt then that unless I write something down, even though I was unsure about some aspects of the case, I was likely to spend the rest of the night thinking and rethinking about Gregg's murder. That would be wasting even more time on this case, time I could hardly afford.

It was around nine in the evening when I finished my report, photocopied it and distributed the copies into the departmental mailboxes of the committee members, and Professors Czerny and Turner.

My report was just three pages long. I summarized the information I had gathered from talking to different people. Gregg was an uninspired student, an opportunist at best. He was not under stress at the time of his death. On the contrary, he seemed to have been unusually up-beat just then, talking about wealth he was about to receive and an intended career change. It was unlikely that anyone under those conditions would commit suicide. I concluded my report by stating that there were strong reasons to believe that Gregg was murdered and that the matter should be further investigated by the police. I did not mention the theory of exchanged cyanide bottles, for I did not want to introduce ideas that I might be called on to defend and thus lose even more time on the project.

I felt a burden lift off my shoulders when the report was completed and delivered to various mailboxes in the department.

*   *   *

"This much, why have you given?" That would be the translation of what I said to Meera in *Telugu.* I was pointing at the plate with masala chicken, cabbage curry, hot mango chutney and rice, and the bowl of gulab jaman – all of which Meera set before me on the dining table. I had bicycled home even though it was dark and Meera would have come with the car to take me and my bike home. I wanted a slow transition between work and home, a few minutes to forget my disappointing activities in the department.

"Because you haven't eaten your evening meals yet," she said. Meera made no distinction between breakfast, lunch, dinner or supper. The plural meals referred to every one of them. I tried to correct her usage without any success

I had called Meera from the department, when I realized that I would be working late to finish the report and, after briefing her on my day's activities, told her that I'd have my supper in the cafeteria. But Meera had known all along that I would not eat until I had finished the report and then I'd rather come home than go to a cafeteria.

I returned half the food on my plate to the proper dishes, before starting to eat. Meera served herself a small portion of rice and cabbage curry and sat across from me. I surmised that it was her second meal. There was a time when she would not eat until I had come home and finished my dinner. I had objected to the observance of that Indian custom, which I consider quite uncivilized. These days she would eat a portion and wait for the rest until I had returned.

"Jay went to sleep early. He finished his homework and wrote the letter to Ammaji," Meera informed me. I was glad that I wouldn't have to prod him into writing his grandmother.

A very comforting thought crossed my mind then, and not for the first time. I had been working, often under barely tolerable conditions, sometimes under trying circumstances, rarely with satisfaction but more often with vague anguish, alternating between hope of finding a better tomorrow and fear of being stuck in a morass of meaningless research. I had been doing all this not for the contingent fame and fortune of a distant tomorrow but for the welcoming reception at home every day. I looked at Meera appreciatively for welcoming me home.

And the two cats, Ding and Dong, waiting impatiently for their share of the chicken, made it an even better welcome.

Chapter 11

Ink and Paper

I was locking my bicycle in front of the chemistry building when I heard Cathy's voice behind me. "Just the man I don't want to see."

When I turned around to face her she said, "Sankar, be prepared. You may get some flak from Professor Czerny."

When Cathy returned to the office, after helping me with the purchase orders, she found Professors Fuller and Czerny in a conference. They wanted to know what Cathy and I had been doing in the business office. She told them of our activities and my theory of the exchanged cyanide bottles. That sent Professor Fuller, as Cathy said, into orbit. I didn't understand why Professor Fuller would be so upset.

"He kept on saying, 'I am the chairman of the committee and all activities must be okayed by me.' Surprisingly, Professor Czerny kept on apologizing for not clearing things up with Professor Fuller before he gave the OK to go ahead with the purchase orders."

"Did you tell them that the cyanide order we found was from Professor Blackwell's group?"

"I had to."

I asked Cathy whether anyone in Professor Blackwell's lab was informed about my theory of the cyanide bottles. If that had been the case, the bottle I was looking for could have been removed before I sneaked into the laboratory.

"I can't be sure but I know Professor Czerny made a few phone calls after I told him about our discovery," Cathy replied.

I was irritated. It looked like Professor Czerny had sabotaged my investigation. It doesn't matter now, I told myself. Your involvement with the committee is over.

*   *   *

I turned the diffusion pump on and poured liquid nitrogen into the cold trap. Another fifteen minutes and the apparatus would be ready for gathering data. If I had been able get my mind off Gregg's case and concentrate on research, I would have gotten useful results by the end of the day. Unfortunately that turned out to be just another hope.

"There you are! Hiding behind a vacuum rack." Professor Fuller's voice rose over the throbbing of the vacuum pump. I didn't think that he would come to the department that early in the morning. I offered him the only chair in the lab, but he preferred to remain standing.

"Can we go over your report now?"

I nodded yes, even though I realized that my approval was not being sought.

"First let me say that I was impressed by the speed with which you did it. I'd give you an A for effort ... But there are some problems with the report, as there usually are with any first attempt, and I must point them out to you. Your style is quite uneven. And you do have difficulties with the articles, as people from your part of the globe usually do, but any reasonable secretary should be able to take care of that problem. We wouldn't worry about that ... But there are two things that really bother me about this report. First, it is - how should I say it - lopsided, unbalanced. You talked only to those people who felt that Gregg was under no pressure. You did not give any weight to the opposite view."

"I talked to the people who knew Gregg best. There aren't that many who were familiar with him."

"Well, you should talk to more students. Talk to grad students who took courses with Gregg. Talk to those who graded exams with him. He might have told them of his feelings toward the faculty or his research supervisor. I never met a grad student who didn't harbor some deep seated grudge against the faculty. It's a perfectly justified feeling, as long as it doesn't get obsessive. If it gets obsessive then it may lead to very unpleasant behavior and possibly even to suicide."

Much as I was annoyed, I tried to remain polite. Why should I work to prove Professor Fuller's theories of grad students' feelings? Obviously he was not willing to accept my suggestion that Gregg had been feeling no pressure while pretending to pursue graduate studies. I had already decided to quit the committee at an appropriate moment, but I also wanted to maintain good relations with Professor Fuller. So I decided not to challenge his views on how grad students feel. Instead I simply said, "It would take up a lot of my time to conduct that many interviews."

"Not necessarily. I could ask Martha to prepare a list of five or six students who could give you a balanced view on Gregg. As efficient as you are, you could probably finish interviewing and writing in a few hours."

I didn't want to tell him that I had no intentions of doing that. "Maybe I should start with you," I said trying to keep my irritation from showing.

"Why me?"

"After all Gregg came here to work with you."

"Who told you that?"

I didn't want to cause any trouble to John Spikes by mentioning his name. "Something in Gregg's folder led me to that conclusion."

"I'm afraid you're wrong. I go on several recruiting trips in any given semester. Believe me, it costs me more than what this university reimburses. But I do it for the department and not to pack my lab with grad students. When I recruit grad students they often feel obligated to work under my direction. But I make it clear to them that they are free to choose any professor in the department. Indeed I insist that they talk to at least three other professors before I let them join my group. I knew from the beginning that Gregg needed firmer guidance than I was willing to give my students. Hence I suggested that he join Blackwell's group. I really don't know what happened after that. He never even came to see me. I certainly would not have suggested that he join Turner's group. Let me put it this way. If Blackwell is to my right, Frank Turner is to my extreme left. I knew from the beginning that Gregg and Frank would make a bad team."

Before I could come up with a polite excuse for terminating the conversation, Professor Fuller continued.

"Now my second complaint. It's about the paragraph before the last. Do you recall what you wrote? Let me read the critical sentence. 'From these considerations, one cannot escape the conclusion that Gregg was poisoned by someone who had access to the cyanide bottles in different chemistry laboratories.' That just about ruined the credibility of the whole report. You just can't say such things casually."

Credibility! What a strange word! I said, "Well, my whole thesis was that Gregg had been quite happy, upbeat and looking forward to a better future. Even the letter terminating his appointment, which I assume he had received, didn't bother him. Doesn't it then follow that he wasn't likely to kill himself."

"Yes and no. A graduate student is an unpredictable animal. One moment he acts as though he's going to devote his whole life to a research project and you trust him with your most important idea. The next moment he runs off with a pretty bimbo and leaves expensive equipment in shambles. And we know that even those who appear to be well adjusted and cheerful often go through intensive counseling. For all I know Gregg could have been one of those who deny every troubling thought until the last fatal moment."

Professor Fuller looked at me as though he was expecting me to object, but I kept quiet.

"The real offence here," he said as he pointed to my report, "is that you're stepping into someone else's territory. It's up to the police to come up with such a conclusion. Sankar, look at it this way. I'm a chemist, of sorts. That's my territory. It's not a physical territory, nevertheless it's a territory. If a police detective comments on my research in chemistry, he loses his credibility. Besides, he'd irritate me since he encroached on what I consider as my rightful territory. Sankar, if you want to survive in today's intensely organized society, you will never step into others' territory and you will never let anyone step into yours ... You see what I mean?"

I wondered whether he was saying that I stepped out of bounds when, without his consent, I searched through the purchase orders and again when I entered Professor Blackwell's lab. He undoubtedly suspected that I had searched through Professor Blackwell's lab.

"Sankar, I'm sorry that I have to be so negative. I cannot bring this report up for discussion in our next meeting."

I said that I had no objections. I thought of saying that for all I cared at that moment he could burn the report, but controlled myself.

Professor Fuller did not leave right away. He inquired about the research problem I was pursuing and how I had been progressing. Before he left he invited me and Meera to a party at his house that evening. Basil Fox, a well-known researcher from a prestigious university, was visiting the department. The Fullers had invited several faculty and post-docs for cocktails and finger food.

"You must come. No excuses will be accepted," he said as he left.

Territories! What an interesting concept! I suppose that modern life consists of invisible boundaries between abstract territories. I, for one, coming from where I did without money or burning talent, had been stepping across the boundaries to make a living, only to be pushed back.

*   *   *

It took a great deal of effort to get my mind back on the research project. An hour later, when I was about to introduce the sample into the vacuum line, Cathy Quintaro barged into the lab saying, "Sankar, Dr. Czerny wants to see you immediately."

She waited until I lodged the sample tube securely and went around the vacuum rack. I knew then that I'd be losing another day.

Professor Czerny stuck his head out of his office and said, "Sankar, could you wait. I'm on a conference call for GEDEC." He closed the door before I could reply.

"That's Gadsden Economic Development Council," Cathy enlightened me, as she handed me a thick glossy folder. "Professor Czerny is one of the founding members. They want to bring more environmentally safe and high-paying industries into our state."

I absent mindedly examined the many charts, graphs and tables in the GEDEC brochure for about fifteen minutes before Professor Czerny came out.

"Gregg's mother and step-father are in town," he said as we stood in front of his office. "Staying at the University Inn. I'll be taking them out for dinner tonight – as a goodwill gesture. I wonder whether you could find me some memento that I could take along to give them."

"A memento?"

"A keepsake from the lab for Gregg's parents. His lab notebook perhaps, if it can be spared, any photographs of Gregg in the lab, or any small gadget he built that is not being used. Look around. I just want to give something to the parents that will remind them of Gregg."

Even though I agreed to do it, I couldn't quite see how any item from the lab would make an appropriate memento.

"Can you let me know before four this afternoon. That'll give me time to look for an alternative, if you can't find something nice."

"Sure."

"Oh, do check with Frank Turner before you go looking around in the lab. It's always a good policy to get the supervisor's okay."

I thought of asking whether he had called Professor Blackwell or his associates the previous day and warned them of my planned search for the cyanide bottle. But before I could phrase my question Professor Czerny slipped back into his office saying that he had an important phone call to make. He closed the door firmly behind him.

"He's going at maximum warp speed today," Cathy commented as I left.

*   *   *

"For what am I supposed to give permission?" Professor Turner wanted to know. We were sitting at a table next to a window in the second floor cafeteria. Professor Turner had noticed me while I was checking the mail and had suggested that I join him for lunch. I was anxious to accept. I had not seen him since he had stormed out of his office on Tuesday afternoon. Ever since receiving Professor Turner's memo accusing Professor Czerny of trying to abridge his academic freedom, I had been looking forward for an occasion to explain my intention to quit the committee while maintaining cordial relations with each faculty member.

"I'd like to go through Gregg's desk and lab bench," I said without mentioning that I had already done that. Professor Turner's lunch, he kept the dishes on the tray, consisted of a large bowl of soup, a turkey-avocado sandwich, pecan pie and a twelve ounce cup of black coffee. Mine was relatively modest – three bean salad in a Chinese paper box and a small coffee. I remembered then that the peanut butter sandwich from Monday was still on my bookshelf, on its fourth day of fighting entropy. Forgetting it for so long was an indication, I thought, of how hectic my recent activities had been.

"Why do you need my permission?"

I explained my mission and Professor Czerny's specific instructions that I should get Professor Turner's prior permission.

"I don't think you'll find anything useful. Look around anyway."

I had been worried about my lagging lab work and Professor Turner's fiery memo and I wondered how I could bring those topics into discussion without angering him. I had not been able to do a single experiment during the previous four days. Since I was paid on Professor Turner's grant, he had every reason to be cross at me for spending time away from the lab bench. He had given me permission to be on the committee but, like me, he probably underestimated its impact on my research. Now that he knew one of the goals of the committee was to embarrass him, I was worried that he would be very displeased with my committee involvement and lack of progress in the lab.

I was also bothered by Professor Turner's memo to the committee. During a previous conversation he had said, in no uncertain terms, that Gregg showed no promise in the lab. Yet in his memo he stated that Gregg had been a very promising researcher. He also stated in his memo that he had much less per-capita lab space than the other faculty. Even though I work in crowded quarters, the other part of Professor Turner's lab was quite spacious and was more than sufficient for all his projects. What were Professor Turner's intentions in writing that memo? Had he been expecting me to stay on the committee and defend his claims? How could I do that, even if I were willing, against the far superior skills and endowed powers of Professors Czerny and Fuller?

"Ah, Sankar! Can you take my three o'clock discussion? That's for tomorrow, Friday." Professor Turner interrupted my thoughts. "You don't have to prepare anything. Just put in an appearance."

"Yes," I said, unable to think of a good excuse. "What is the course?"

"Chem 100. It's a one semester course for those who don't want to learn chemistry. Cosmetics and Park Management majors besides cowboys from Ag school.. No science or math prerequisites."

"What should I cover?"

"Nothing. Just answer if there are any questions. You will probably see ten out of the two hundred registered in the class. If there are any questions at all they will be on the basics like atoms, molecules and chemical symbols. I hadn't covered much of anything in the course so far. We've had only two lectures. The regular class meets Tuesdays and Thursdays."

Much as I was not anxious to take up another additional non-research duty, I was glad that Professor Turner had asked me to do this small favor. Now I felt that I could bring up my worries.

"I'm thinking of quitting the committee," I said.

"Why?"

"I don't want to be caught in the cross-fire."

"Are you worried about my memo?"

"Yes."

"Don't be. I am not counting on you to defend my position in the committee meetings. I wouldn't defend it myself."

I was puzzled.

"Had Czerny ever bothered to ask me,

I'd have recommended terminating Gregg's appointment. And I'm not even anxious to hold on to that barn of a lab and the small broom closet you use for your experiments. I'd be glad to exchange them both for a single medium size lab."

I couldn't conceal my puzzlement. "I don't understand."

"What don't you understand?"

"Your memo. When I read it I got the exact opposite message."

"Sure, you did."

I expected Professor Turner to elaborate. Instead he said, "This pie is very good. I'm going to get another piece."

"Let me explain the two principles of academic politics," he said when he returned with the second piece of pie and a second cup of coffee. "The first is: never give up anything voluntarily, even the stuff you absolutely don't want. Even your old notebooks with more scribbles than sentences. You lose your ability to bargain. If I readily agree to move into a smaller lab or don't protest that my student was fired without consulting me, I end up losing far more than I can afford. Now Czerny and his compadres know that if they try to do anything without negotiating first I'll bring the matter up in some university-wide committee. Believe me, they are quite aware that it would delay anything they want to do for more years than they are likely to live."

I wondered what Professor Turner's negotiating terms were. What was he willing to give up in exchange? It seemed inappropriate to ask, but he volunteered the information anyway.

"I want Czerny to come up with money to remodel a medium size lab. Replace the old wiring with modern outlets, install high-performance hoods, put in really decent lab benches and a few other things like that. Then I'll give up the big lab and your area. I also want the department to pay for a post-doc for six months or a grad student for a year. Otherwise I'll complain that Czerny abridged my academic freedom by firing one of my students without consulting me. I'll also put the blame on Czerny for Gregg's suicide. You have to be tough with these guys."

It was indeed a strange world into which I had been seeking an entry.

"By the way," Professor Turner continued. "The fight is between me and the head and his toadies. I don't expect you to be involved in it even if my memo comes up for discussion in the committee."

I was delighted to hear that. The gentle sun came out from behind the dark clouds – metaphorically speaking – and I felt comfortable enough to ask, "You said there are two principles of academic politics. What is the second?"

"When a squid is threatened, it releases an ink-like substance in all directions. The resulting opacity and confusion protects the creature. When a faculty member perceives danger, he or she spews out ink and paper. Lots and lots - and very rapidly."

With those comments he got up and darted toward the exit with the agility of an animal running down its prey. I gulped the dregs of my coffee and followed him, marveling at the strange rituals of the tribe.

*   *   *

It was quite clear that Gregg had done very little productive work in the lab. The top of his lab bench was covered with a thin coat of Gadsden dust. There was no indication that he had used the bench top for mixing chemicals, putting together an apparatus, or even for spreading out data sheets to be pored over. At one end of that unused bench stood the ill-designed optical sector, too large to go with any of the instruments in Professor Turner's lab. The electrical connections, instead of being safely tucked away, went all around the device, like the blood vessels of a patient on a surgical table. There would be no mystery about his death had he turned on that sector – he would have been electrocuted instantaneously.

The shelves under the lab bench contained the usual glassware and a motley collection of tools. I wondered whether he put that stuff there just to lay claim to the space. One of the drawers under the lab bench contained a few notebooks, some dating back to his undergraduate days. None of them were lab note books used for recording procedures and data. The other drawer contained several magazines, some still in their sealed plastic jackets. It was becoming obvious that I would not find a suitable memento for Professor Czerny. However, I wasn't willing to give up yet.

The small desk where Gregg's body had been found was squeezed between a bookshelf lab and the double doors, barely clearing the door to the next room. I had gotten the keys from a drawer in that desk earlier. Nevertheless I continued to search the desk and its contents for something I could give Dr. Czerny. The top of the desk was clear except for a few scattered pencils, a paperback dictionary, an old edition of the *Handbook of Chemistry and Physics* and Gregg's lab notebook. I leafed through the almost empty book - there were only two entries. One of them was a list of experiments Gregg was supposed to do and the other, a list of supplies he needed for his research. I had no reason to believe that he had either attempted the experiments or even ordered the necessary supplies.

Every corner of the lab carries the insignia of the researcher assigned to that space. You can tell a lot about that researcher by just looking at his or her lab bench and desk. Except for the sight of the ugly, unsafe optical sector on the bench and three crumpled scientific articles in his desk, I would have concluded that Gregg was a figment of somebody's wild imagination. I was surprised to note that the articles were thoroughly read and heavily underlined, with comments and cross references in the margin. That's what I usually do before I start a research project: take the important articles and go over them line by line. I almost believed that those dog-eared articles were an indication that Gregg was getting serious about research. However, to my greater surprise I found those were Professor Richard Blackwell's articles. What was Gregg doing studying articles not relevant to his present research? He should have been concentrating on Professor Turner's articles. Perhaps the papers were leftovers from his days in Professor Blackwell's lab. If that were the case, it only showed that Gregg had not done anything since he joined Professor Turner's group.

Unfortunately, my speculation did not stop there but raised a disturbing thought. Was Gregg still working for Professor Blackwell while pretending to be Professor Turner's student? Was he planted in Professor Turner's lab as a spy? Was he a double agent? What was there to spy? Professor Turner wasn't involved in classified research or in industrial consulting. The idea of spying was far fetched; but then everything about this case was far fetched and the idea couldn't be dismissed summarily. Nevertheless I decided not to think about the case and report my negative results to Professor Czerny.I started toward the main office wondering how I could convince Professor Czerny that I had indeed gone over Gregg's lab corner thoroughly and hadn't been able to find anything that could be a memento. I didn't want him to think that I had ignored his request. Well, it turned out that I didn't have to worry. Cathy Quintaro found me in the corridor and said, "Sankar, don't go on searching in Gregg's lab."

An explanation followed. Since my last conversation with him, Professor Turner had changed his mind. He had called Professor Czerny to tell him that he would not allow even a piece of scratch paper to be taken out of his lab. That made Professor Czerny mad enough to dictate a nasty letter to Professor Turner.

"Like a bunch of wild kids. When will they grow up?"

I knew the answer to Cathy's question but there was no reason to say it. Undoubtedly she knew it too.

I drifted toward my bicycle, glad that I didn't have to face either of the professors at that moment.

Chapter 12

An Academic Party

I thought you wanted nothing to do with the profs. Now you're going to party with them," Zach Setlow commented. He was then stripping a table, perhaps an antique, of its badly worn finish.

"I can explain," I said without intending to go into any explanation at that time.

"You don't have to. You are not going to rest until you know the truth about Gregg."

"My husband is always like that, Zach. He complains everyday, but he doesn't quit."

"Don't worry, Meera. He will probably find a clue or two at the party. Go and enjoy yourselves."

We had come to drop Jay with Zach on our way to the party at the Fullers' house. The meetings with Professors Fuller, Czerny and Turner, and the search through Gregg's desk and lab bench - all these unusual activities - had warped my sense of time and I had forgotten to call Meera about the party. She wasn't pleased when I had insisted that we could not and should not miss the party. She had protested by saying that it would be very difficult to find a baby sitter on such short notice. My suggestion, that Jay was old enough to be left alone, had fallen on deaf years. I had called, at Meera's insistence, several youth in the neighborhood, but every one of them said no for sitting past ten, this being a school night. After I had exhausted the possibilities in the neighborhood, I called Zach.

To my great relief Zach had said, "Bring him over. I have to go into town in the morning and I can drop him at the school then."

Zach lived in the middle of what looked like a mesquite forest, twenty miles southeast of the city center. It was not an easy place to find after sunset. But once we got there I felt we were on a different planet. The dark trunks and the leafless branches of mesquite trees against the diffuse moonlight gave a magical quality to the landscape. A few miles to the south, the San Rafael Mountains formed an impressive backdrop to Zach's property. I thought it would be nice to take a leisurely stroll on the two mile trail from his house to the Rio Camello Wash, particularly in the moonlight. There would be no time for that today. I was anxious to get to the party at a reasonable time. Meera didn't share my view and spent another half hour discussing real estate with Zach and inquiring what he had been doing on his property.

"I'm going to drag Jay out of bed at the crack of dawn and show him the wildlife around here. You guys have a good time," Zach said as I turned the car around in the narrow driveway, avoiding the cacti and boulders.

*   *   *

I assumed, correctly, that the woman who let us in was Mrs. Fuller. She wore a long silk skirt with a bold magenta pattern and a light pink blouse.

"You must be Sankar," she greeted me with a broad smile. "My husband said a lot about the good work you've been doing. By the way, I'm Jane Fuller." Before I could answer, she turned to Meera and said, "Oh Dear! I've forgotten your name."

"Meera, Mrs. Fuller."

"What a pretty name. I like it. Like your sari too. Just call me Jane. We don't have any formalities here. You know this party is supposed to be quite informal, too. Sankar, just go around and introduce yourself. Drinks are that-a-way." Waving her arm toward the back of the room, Mrs. Fuller disappeared into the crowd dragging Meera along.

"I'm sorry that we are late," I managed to say before they vanished.

"Don't worry. The party is just getting started," Mrs. Fuller called over her shoulder.

We had to drive nearly thirty miles from Zach's place to the Fullers' house, from the southeast to the northwest side of Gadsden. As I tried to hurry I realized that driving to an unknown destination in Gadsden after nightfall was a very challenging experience. Street lights did not exist and the street signs - two inch plates with long Spanish names starting with Calle, Camino or Avenida - were almost invisible. The edges of the roads, unmarked by pavement or white lines, blended gradually into ditch and desert. Mail boxes showed no indication of the house number or who lived there. It was close to ten when we presented ourselves to Jane Fuller.

The living room and what was called the Gadsden room - a living room for informal occasions - were packed with people I had often seen in the chemistry building, but whose names remained unfamiliar to me. The guests formed small groups and everyone was talking, quite animated. There were more people in the well-lit yard, beyond the glass sliding door.

Unlike Meera, who quickly makes friends with strangers and talks with ease about nylon saris, the Taj Mahal, Tandoori cooking and the intricate machines of the American kitchen, I do not feel comfortable outside the lab. I have always been at a loss for suitable topics of conversation. Men talked about sports – which never interested me; about academic politics for which, since it controlled my livelihood, I had developed a strong distaste and deep-seated fear; or about cars, cameras and other consumer goods, which remained beyond my means and alien to my temperament.

I felt particularly uneasy about this party. My mind was still on the recent events. Zach and Meera were only partly right. It wasn't the truth that I was obsessed with. I was after the facts. Facts may never reveal the complete truth. Indeed we may have to invent theories and scenarios to connect the facts and in that process truth may even be buried. Yet without facts there is not the slightest chance of getting close to truth.

However, I wasn't in a mood to discuss facts (I had none that mattered) or theories which I could not defend. I stood very self-consciously in the corridor, unable to move, approximately where Jane Fuller had left me, pretending to examine abstract blotches of color on a piece of canvas.

"Sankar!" I heard the familiar voice of Professor Fuller. "If you stare at that painting any longer, I'll demand that you take it home."

I was glad to see someone familiar, even though I sincerely wished it was someone other than the chairman of the committee.

"You must meet our distinguished visitor, Professor Fox. A really charming scientist. Immensely talented." With those comments, Professor Fuller led me to the fireplace – there was no fire and no need for one – and pushed me between two people in a large group.

"Basil, you have to meet our detective-in-residence, Sankar," Professor Fuller addressed the visitor in a loud voice. "I should actually call him Sankarlock, considering the way he looks for subtle clues. Since you're a detective story buff, Basil, I thought you'd enjoy talking to each another."

I felt sick. I wasn't in the mood to receive criticism, or compliments for that matter, and particularly not criticism that sounded like a compliment. I shook hands with the distinguished visitor, remembering to make the handshake firm. Professor Fox was of medium height, with a tense, square face and a suggestion of a beer belly. He wore a dark suit and a reddish tie - the only one in the crowd wearing both tie and jacket. I couldn't help notice the looks of great admiration he was receiving from everyone around him.

"I understand you have a case of suicide in your department," commented Professor Fox.

"It looks that way. But I am not completely convinced." Now that I had been called Sankarlock, I didn't see any reason to withhold my unproven theory.

"That's interesting. Jim said he was quite sure it was suicide."

"I must admit, Professor Fox, that it's probably impossible to prove otherwise. But, for my money, it isn't suicide." I was surprised at my own boldness.

"Just Basil ... please. No old-fashioned formalities. What makes you think it isn't a suicide?"

"Gregg Westover - that's the name of the fellow - lived a life free of worries and free of scruples. I talked to people who knew him well. Gregg was in an optimistic mood, expecting to acquire some money and start a new life elsewhere. He had no reason to kill himself."

"You never know what's really worrying a grad student. Besides I don't think anyone needs a reason to quit this life."

Professor Fox obviously had made up his mind. I didn't want to prolong the conversation on Gregg Westover, so I said, "That's why it is difficult to know what really happened," hoping that we would move on to a different topic.

"I think we probably have more experience with suicides in our department than you have here. I don't believe that your students go through the same high pressure curriculum as ours."

I wondered whether there was, at that moment, some grad student in psychology or sociology, doing a thesis project correlating suicide rates and suicidal tendencies with the supposedly high standards of some institutions.

"You do get some of the best grad students, don't you?" Someone from the crowd said.

"Yes. I'd say their caliber is the same as those going to Harvard or Caltech."

"How do you manage to do that?" Another unidentified voice asked.

"It isn't easy, I tell you. There simply aren't enough competent students who want to go to grad school these days, but ever since Brent became the chairman, we've followed an aggressive policy of recruiting. We contact outstanding undergrads in their junior year and get them to visit us. Wine and dine them, figuratively speaking. We then try to hook them by giving summer financial support and bonuses of one sort or the other. I'm not on the committee. So I don't know all the details, but the committee spends a great deal of time and money recruiting. It's a full time job for two secretaries and at least quarter time work for the faculty on the committee."

"There used to be a distinction between football and science," the fellow next to me muttered in my ear. He was a total stranger to me.

"Sankar - did I get your name right?" continued Professor Fox. "Here are some impressive statistics for you. One of my post-docs estimated that one's chance of committing suicide is thirty per cent, if he or she works for Brent. The chance of getting divorced is sixty per cent. The odds of getting divorced and also committing suicide are, curiously, twenty-five per cent. How's that for an interesting study of probabilities?"

Interesting?

"One of my grad students killed himself a couple of years ago - shot himself in the head. I never found out what really was at the root. He was doing OK in the lab. Not the brightest I ever had, but competent. I think it was the bimbo-factor more than the research that flipped him. The student newspaper blamed me for it though - without any facts to support their theory."

Facts. Yes, I needed facts to support my theory. I thought I could quit the case after I finished writing the report, and again after the sermon from Professor Fuller on territories while I was concentrating on my work in the lab. It took me some time to realize I couldn't. Perhaps finding facts in this case was my inalienable duty as Meera would say. I might try, but I wouldn't be able to liberate myself from my inalienable duty.

Many people began to talk simultaneously, but Professor Fox spoke above the din.

"I think the newspaper missed the point. We live in a difficult times, unfortunately. There is lots of pressure on everybody. We are just inches away from ecological disasters. The specter of mushroom clouds spreading across the planet has not diminished, now that many under-developed countries have nuclear technology and at least a minimum expertise to make atomic bombs. Population is growing beyond our capabilities to produce food, particularly in Sankar's native land and other third world countries," Professor Fox said without looking at me. "Resources are dwindling at an alarming rate while pollution is getting intolerable. Governments do not seem to have the will or wisdom to support research in critical areas, research that would help us solve these problems. It's a bleak picture. Very bleak picture indeed. Some people just can't take it. It's too much for them. I've been accused of being totally callous for saying this, but the truth is we can't do anything for people who aren't tough enough and resourceful enough to be able to live in this highly competitive world."

The fellow who had whispered in my ear had left sometime back, but the rest of the crowd listened with attention. I wondered what relevance, if any, Professor Fox's global perspective had to do with Gregg Westover's untimely death.

*   *   *

I left Professor Fox and his coterie of admirers and wandered from one group to another without much luck in attracting either attention or interest. Professor Findlay, dressed better than usual in a white guayabera shirt and dark dress slacks, was surrounded by several grad students who were almost shouting at each other. Professor Czerny was sitting on a sofa, talking to three professors while drawing sketches on a pad of paper. Obviously his visit with Gregg's parents had been a short one. As I had expected, Professor Turner was nowhere to be seen. I thought I saw Niles Baxter in the crowd but he vanished before I could corner him.

After eating a dozen mini-chimis with guacamole sauce and filling a large glass with a soft drink, I looked around again for a suitable group to join. Spotting Professor Blackwell in the company of three - a young man and a couple - I went over to meet him. I wanted to tell him about the article reprints I had found in Gregg's desk. He, however, was distinctly displeased with my presence and turned away as soon as I approached him.

I realized that I had interrupted the conversation since the fellow with his arm around the young woman's waist prompted, "You were talking about your trip, Dr.Blackwell."

"Oh, yes. I'll be leaving in a couple of hours. Taking a red eye flight. I'll be back midnight Sunday. Actually it would be Monday morning technically."

I was determined to join the conversation. "Where are you going?" I asked.

"San Diego. I'm collaborating with a biochemist there on a project," he said without looking at me and continued to address the other three. "As I was saying, that gives me very little time to do any science. I wanted to leave Gadsden on Monday so that I'd have a full week for research, but I couldn't get anyone in the faculty to take my classes. Czerny, I can't figure him out, wouldn't let grad students sub. Evidently I used grad students to sub too often last semester. If I did, it was for a good cause. My question is: if you don't have opportunities to travel and collaborate with other scientists how are you going to keep up with the changes in your field? How can you possibly do cutting-edge research? The powers that be in this institution have to decide once for all. Do they want a first rate university or a junior college?"

I decided to be a mere spectator since it appeared that Professor Blackwell was not going to turn in my direction.

"Somebody has to do the teaching. After all we do charge the students tuition," the young woman said.

"Yes. There's no question about it," Professor Blackwell said vehemently. "To me teaching is training grad students and post-docs, not what goes on in the classrooms. I spend no less than twelve hours a day, seven days a week teaching research skills to my graduate students. That's real teaching. We have to ask ourselves whether we want a first rate research university in this state or not. If we do, we have to allow the productive faculty to teach their graduate students and find adjunct faculty to conduct the classes for the hordes of unprepared and uninterested undergrads. I say give absolute freedom for research faculty so that they can aggressively go after promising ideas."

"But you are paid, supposedly, for teaching and not for research," she continued.

"Nonsense. I bring in more research money than anybody else in the department. The overhead on that alone keeps a couple of administrators employed."

Dr. Blackwell had a point there, but I didn't want to add my two cents. The lady in our company, however, seemed determined to challenge him. "You wouldn't be able to get those grants except for the huge support the university gives you," she said. "The university pays research-active professors fat salaries, gives them lab space and every facility in the world. This is supposed to help the students when, in fact, professors don't want to have anything to do with the students."

"I didn't get your name," Dr. Blackwell tried to slow down the onslaught.

"Stephanie."

"Stephanie is a grad student in medical anthropology, Dr. Blackwell," her date added.

"Stephanie, I simply don't see your point. If we don't maintain leadership in research we are going to fall behind Europe and Japan."

"Don't you need well-educated undergraduates to maintain that leadership? Who is going to prepare them, if people like you don't want to teach?"

"You are changing the subject, Stephanie."

"Not really. How about graduate students? Don't you need competent graduate students to maintain the leadership in research?"

"Of course, we do."

I thought of pointing out that they, the professors, also need competent post docs for maintaining that leadership, but I was enjoying the argument too much to interrupt.

"How are you going to get competent graduate students if you downgrade undergraduate teaching?"

"Who said anything about downgrading undergraduate teaching?"

"You don't have to say it. You are doing it."

I noticed a few heads turning our direction.

"What the hell do you mean?" Dr. Blackwell shouted.

"None of you really want to teach lower division courses. Most of the times you are chasing grant money. You want freedom from teaching to do it. You said a minute ago that what goes on in the classroom doesn't matter. So why do you even offer courses and pretend you are helping the students?"

I thought Dr. Blackwell was going to punch her. His fists were clenched and his face was distorted with intense rage. He continued to shout angrily.

"Stephanie, I am talking about the need for first-class research and you are talking about an entirely different thing. If you have a complaint about undergraduate education, take it up with the university administration. Or better yet with school boards."

There was complete silence for a moment.

"I better go and see Basil before he leaves," Dr. Blackwell muttered, turning away from the group abruptly.

*   *   *

"My husband," Meera said pointing me to Laura Blackwell.

"We have met before," I said.

"Yes, we have."

The two were sitting across from each other at the dining table next to the kitchen.

"Sorry to interrupt your conversation," I said.

"Don't be. I suppose you got an earful from my husband about lack of support for research."

"Something like that."

"That was the topic of conversation when I first met him. He was in graduate school then. And that has been the topic of conversation ever since."

"That's the impression I got from our two meetings."

"Richard is driven. He can't wait until he gets there ahead of schedule."

"It must be hard on you."

"Not really. We complement each other."

"That's good."

"We have been a team ever since we met. I know Richard tends to turn people off, but deep down he has a good heart. I think he'll mellow once he gets a tenured appointment."

"I understand it's almost settled."

"Almost but not quite. The provost got into trouble last year for recommending promotion to someone in physics. It turned out the man had shares in a company involved in shady deals. I suspect the provost is looking into Richard's contacts with companies. Perhaps you don't know, but Richard gets a lot of support from a few companies. That's what keeps his group afloat."

"He has a very large group, doesn't he?"

"I think the largest in the department now."

"It must be a strain on you as well, perhaps indirectly."

"Not indirectly. Directly. I keep track of what his graduate students are doing, make sure they meet the deadlines. I edit their papers. Most of them can't write a decent sentence. The more graduate students Richard signs in, the more work for me."

"Professor Blackwell is a very lucky man," Meera said.

"That's not all I do. I keep Richard's papers in order. I am his contact with grant administrators and sometimes even with other faculty. I bring him his lunch and snacks when he wants. Of course, I cook and feed him on time at home."

"You are like a Hindu wife, Laura. That's what our religion teaches us. Husband is more important than all the gold and riches," Meera was quick to add.

"More in mythology than in reality," I couldn't help saying.

"I don't mind being a full-time assistant, counselor and cook for Richard. We are building a career together. Once he's established we will start a family. The way I feel, we are working for our common future. I don't like these women who compete with their husbands and complain about divorces. If you can't be part of a team, you shouldn't be married in the first place."

I moved away quietly while Laura Blackwell and Meera extended their discussion of marriage and wifely duties.

*   *   *

Some time later I saw Laura Blackwell in the company of a professor I often saw in the corridors of the chemistry building. I didn't know his name or specialty.

"Sankar," she called out to me, "come and join us."

I was about to introduce myself to the professor when Laura said, "Sankar, Jim Fuller said that you think Gregg Westover was murdered. Is that true?"

I had been trying to banish thoughts of Gregg and the committee and get back to my research. So I said, "It was just a passing thought."

"So you don't think Gregg was poisoned?"

"I didn't say that."

"What is it? Homicide or suicide? You can't have it both ways," the professor said. I didn't like his tone which reminded me of the questioning in oral exams.

"I can't be certain without more information."

"But why did you even think it could be homicide in the first place. Did you have any clues?" Laura Blackwell asked in a far more polite tone.

It was clear that I could not banish the ghost of Gregg Westover. I didn't want to mention my failed attempts to find the bottle of cyanide in Professor Blackwell's laboratory. I said, "From what I gathered talking to people around, Gregg was not a sensitive person. Thick-skinned. I don't think it is likely that somebody like that would commit suicide."

"Looks to me, you are theorizing without facts. A dangerous habit I tell my students to avoid," the professor said.

"I'd think that Gregg was exactly the type that would commit suicide," Laura Blackwell said.

I was willing to accept her hypothesis at that moment and move on.

"Sankar," she continued. "I know the guy quite well since he was in Richard's group for nearly two semesters. He was sullen and self-centered. Ungrateful to boot. He couldn't get along with anyone. He was the type that feels lonely and depressed but blames everyone else for his troubles. I'd say he was precisely the type that would commit suicide."

"I suppose so," I said to avoid a debate.

*   *   *

"Dr. Sankar, I presume."

I turned around to see a blonde woman with a pointed chin. Dr. Susan Bond wore a tan outfit cut to look like an airplane mechanic's coverall. After some talk about her research and my research - the usual format for conversation between two scientists getting acquainted - she said, "Sankar, you may not be aware of it, but I'm responsible for your being on Gregg Westover's committee."

"I didn't know that."

"Well, Czerny asked me to be on the committee. I had to say no. I am now on as many committees as anyone can reasonably handle. And WIST - that's Women in Science and Technology - takes up a lot of my time. I can't afford to be on any more committees. Anyway, when I saw the second list Czerny made, I was appalled. There wasn't a single woman or minority representative on the list. I said to Czerny that's ridiculous, simply ridiculous, in this day and age. That's when he started looking at post-doc files since there aren't that many women or minorities on the faculty. I'm sure that's how he found your name."

I wondered whether Susan Bond thought that she had done me a favor by insisting on minority representation.

"I've never been on a committee like this," I said. I did not want to thank her for being instrumental in getting me on the committee. And I did not want to tell her the truth that I was quite uncomfortable with it.

"You probably didn't have the opportunity."

I had thought, in the beginning, that it was an opportunity. Now I would be glad if the committee work did not make me lose my job.

"I want to get minorities and women into every committee. I mean every committee - no exceptions."

I couldn't have missed the zeal in her words.

"We, minorities and women," continued Dr. Bond, "don't understand social dynamics, the way power flows between groups, units and persons. We think that education and training will get us to where we want to go. Education and training are essential. I grant you that. All that work you do, getting education and training, only gets your foot in the door. That's it. Nothing more. After that you have to join the dynamic process, if you want to succeed. You have to work through the committees to get ahead. Look at the dean of our college. I understand that he never published a reviewed article and never even had a major grant. Some years ago he taught a course on cacti for ag majors. That's about the size of his scholarly work. How did he become the highest paid member of the college? How did he get to be in the decision making position?"

I have enough sense not to answer rhetorical questions.

"I bet he got himself into the right committees and worked his way to success. He knew the social dynamics. Had he spent the same amount of time teaching or doing research he would be making one third, or even one fourth, of what he is making now.... And what intellectual heights do you think our esteemed president has scaled?"

I was certain Dr. Susan Bond would have continued her intense crusade, except for the arrival of her husband. "Are you at it again, Dear?" Jonathan Bond put his arm around his wife's shoulder and tugged her toward him. Her expression softened as she looked at the lank figure and she smiled.

"Jonathan is working for a doctorate in anthropology. His interest is the development of scientific thought in primitive societies."

"The way things are going, by the time I finish my doctorate Susan will be a full professor or a dean. I'm very slow."

"You're just working in a difficult area. Original work takes time."

"I am also interested in creative writing. I want to develop a series of novels that are set among various primitive cultures, but reflect the ills of our so called advanced society."

I wanted to ask him to elaborate, but his wife spoke first. "How is your creative writing class anyway?"

"We only had two meetings so far. I missed the second one because I had to drive Mom."

"Is she after you again?"

The Bonds talked about Jonathan's problems with his mother and how she was ruining his schedule. I was feeling left out of the conversation when Jonathan Bond asked me, "Sankar!

Professor Fuller says that you wrote a memo proving that Gregg was murdered. Is that true?"

"That's my hypothesis. Or theory, if you want to call it that. Gregg seemed to be quite happy and satisfied with himself, so I don't see any reason why he would commit suicide."

"None of the other guys considered the possibility of murder?" Susan Bond asked.

"No."

"Jonathan, this illustrates my very point," she said in an excited voice. I didn't see what her point was.

"Sankar," she turned to me and explained, "I want minorities and women on the departmental committees because they provide alternate views to those of white Anglo-Saxon men brainwashed by the dominant culture. You approached the problem of Gregg's death from an entirely different perspective. Because of your widely different background you were able to see that it could be murder rather than suicide. Now that possibility would not have occurred to people like Fuller or Czerny or any of the members of the ruling class. They all grew up in the dominant culture which doesn't accept alternatives."

I didn't know what to say. The thesis that my thinking depended more on my culture, whatever that might be, and less on my originality did not please me.

"You agree then that Gregg was probably murdered," I said. Since she and I, it seemed, came from a different culture than Professor Fuller and his ilk, I thought we could agree on my views.

"I'd have to look at the evidence objectively. From what I was told about pressures on the graduate students it looks like a suicide. But my point is that men raised in the dominant culture are incapable of seeing the whole picture."

It did not sound like a vote of confidence.

*   *   *

"How are you doing, Amigo?" Carlos Quintaro asked shaking my hand vigorously. He was wearing a light blue guayabera shirt, dark blue jeans and cowboy boots. I had spotted him and Cathy standing in a corner, away from the rest of the crowd. Since very few people feel comfortable amidst a gang of chemists, I wasn't surprised that the two kept to themselves.

When Cathy first mentioned that her husband was a graduate student in Hispanic Studies, I had visualized a young man of twenty and odd years, one of Cathy's age. That wasn't the case. With graying hair receding at the temples and a lined forehead, Carlos looked like a man in his late forties.

"Cathy told me you are doing graduate work," I said.

"He is the first to go to college in his family. Maybe even in his whole village. Carlos comes from a small village near Ciudad Obregon," Cathy answered for him.

"No beautiful girls in the village. That's why I went to college," Carlos laughed loudly as he patted Cathy's behind.

Cathy looked mildly displeased.

"How's the investigation going?" she asked me.

Before I could answer, she turned toward Carlos and said, "Sankar thinks that somebody poisoned Gregg, but my boss says it's suicide."

"Suicide or murder," Carlos joined in the conversation. "When a man comes to a bad end it is always because of a woman."

Chapter 13

The Story of Ping

Sometime later, I was alone again - this time in the backyard, breathing the fresh Gadsden air. Winters are usually mild in the Southwest but this year, I was told, the climate was even better. I felt quite comfortable in my light jacket as I walked around the yard trying to identify the plants. The yard was landscaped elegantly for low maintenance, with privet hedges, olive trees and a few native plants I could not identify. Rock borders and gravel paths gave a subtle symmetry to the garden while, at the same time, making it look spacious. The porch contained glazed Mexican pots with more unfamiliar plants in them. The month or so we had been in Gadsden had not given me enough experience to identify the strange and fascinating plants of the region.

I sat on the bench at the corner of the yard. There had been a drizzle earlier and the air was fragrant with a faint smell of creosote. An occasional gentle breeze stirred the wind chimes hung in a nearby tree and made my skin tingle with pleasure.

Meera would like to have a house with a bigger kitchen than we had and an extra bedroom for occasional out of town visitors: a house with a yard where she could grow cilantro, okra,

Andhra egg plant, *gongura* and a few other vegetables that could not readily be bought. Until recently I had been content with apartments as long as there was enough space on the dining table for me to spread the papers I usually brought home, a place to play chess with Jay and go over his homework. Now, having lived in Gadsden for about a month, I too had developed an urge to acquire a house. It would be nice, I thought, to have a vegetable garden and a porch for a ping-pong table. In this part of the world you don't need four walls for protection against the fierce outdoors, except possibly during the summer months. It would be so much more satisfying if I could read in the garden, play chess under a mesquite tree or examine my data on a roughly assembled outdoor table with generous proportions.

Over the years we had saved enough for a down payment on a house, but as Zach Setlow had explained, buying a house would be risky unless we could stay in it for at least two years. If the proposal Professor Turner had been working on was funded and if he and I continued to have a good relationship, I could hope for two or three more years of postdoctoral employment in Gadsden. If the administration decided to hire a new faculty member and if I did get that job, a remote possibility as things stood then, we could hope to be in Gadsden for at least six years. So as I sat in the corner of the Fullers' yard with plants, shrubs and ample open spaces, my thoughts were again on our uncertain future.

"There you are, hiding," I heard Niles Baxter's voice. He was next to the card table near the sliding door pouring a drink into his cup. A grad student and his girl friend sat on the wall talking in low voices. It was nearing midnight and the other guests had already moved indoor.

"Come over here, Sankar," Niles called out.

I didn't want to move from the quiet spot but I knew that Niles would come to me if I continued to stay where I was. Once my thoughts were disturbed it didn't matter who joined whom and so I walked onto the porch.

"Lemme pour you a drink, Sankar. What'll it be?"

He had a silly alcoholic grin on his face and the speech of a drunk. I had had one beer and as many glasses of soda as I could tolerate in one evening. I didn't want any more to drink. "I'll pass."

"Keeping yourself sober, eh? D'yu think I've had one too many?"

I wasn't happy with his company at that moment. So I said, "Maybe."

"You're wrong, Sankar. I'd had three too many or four too many... but I can hold my liquor."

He poured himself a generous portion of scotch. "Boy! I love this stuff ... It makes it worth coming to these god-damned faculty parties."

"What do you think of our visitor, Professor Fox," I said trying to change the topic.

"You don't want to know my opinion. I'll give it anyway. I'm always giving my opinion. Basil Fox is a jerk. He's the type of guy who manages to get lots of grant money by hook or crook. Once you have the money you can just buy talent. And that's all he does. All the work for which he's quote-unquote famous, was done by someone else - a grad student or a post-doc. I don't think Foxy-Woxy ever had one decent scientific idea of his own. Did you ever read any of his papers?"

"No. They aren't relevant to my research."

"They aren't relevant to anybody's research, except they haul in big bucks and big overhead. The only stuff administrators really care about. Overhead and more overhead. That's all these bastards want."

I didn't want to talk about the committee and I didn't want to talk about the overhead and the underhand of the academic finances, but Niles had no intention of quitting the topic.

"Sankar, I had a sudden revelation the other day. Like in a flash. I wondered why I wasn't smart enough to know this all along, why I stupidly spent all my time looking for a university job until I got to this arid, non-aqueous sink hole. It was a great revelation. I should publish it somewhere. An original scholarly communication."

I had no idea what his revelation was and I was afraid to ask.

"Hav'u ever read the story of Ping, Sankar?"

"No."

"You're as bad as the damn Americans. You've no idea of the great cultures of the world."

I took the insult with no comment.

"Sankar, that's supposed to be a joke. You got more culture than those leeches in there." He pointed toward the living room. "I need another drink before I can reveal to you, my trusted friend, what was revealed to me."

Niles twisted his way to the table and poured a drink, spilling as much on the side.

"Where were we? Ah, the story of Ping. These Chinese fishermen are very clever. They put rings around the necks of these birds. What are they called? Oh, yes, the cormorants. Now the cormies go and catch fish except, with those damn rings around their necks, they can't swallow. They can't open their mouths wide enough. So a cormy comes back to the fisherman, he grabs the whole fish, keeps most of it for himself and gives a few tiny bits to the bird. If a cormy wants more it has to go back fishing. Now there's a law written in stone somewhere in the administration building. It says faculty-cormies who do not bring in fish-grants shall perish."

I had been depressed to begin with, thinking about my uncertain future, and now I was even more depressed by the conversation. I was looking for a way of slipping away from Niles' company, when Laura Blackwell came out.

"Hi, Niles. Have you seen Rich."

"Rich who?" he sang in a funny voice.

"Come on, Niles."

"So you don't want to play knock-knock. That's okay. Everything is okay. Everybody is okay. Sankar here is okay. By the way, Laura, have you met Sankar, the super sleuth?"

"Oh, yes."

"I was telling my good friend Sankar that your husband is a good cormy."

"A good what?"

"Cormorant. You need ancient Chinese wisdom to understand that," Niles Baxter said with a silly voice.

She turned to me and said, "Meera invited me to visit. She's going to show me how to put on a sari."

"Sari, that's a good word. Hey, Laura, don't go away. Here is another gem of oriental wisdom." He went into a fit of laughter, occasionally repeating sari, sari. After a while, as he controlled his exuberance, he said, "Laura, what does an Indian say to his wife when the lights're out? I bet you don't know."

"I don't know and I don't care."

"He says, sorry no sari. That's what he says, sorry no sari." He burst into laughter again.

"Niles, please control yourself." She came close to Niles and said, "I know how hard it's on somebody just starting here. The place is a snake-pit. But you can pull through, Niles. Richard did – almost did."

"Yah, but he had you to thank."

His voice sounded very different. It was subdued but clear, with a touch of sadness. I don't think Laura Blackwell heard him as she left our company. Niles continued in the same tone.

"I don't think our poster boy Blackwell deserves her. It's obvious to everyone that he is using her. Wait until he gets tenure. Within a year he'll dump her, find a recent model for bed partner and move on to a bigger and better university."

Niles was lost in his own thoughts and didn't notice as I moved inside.

As I entered the big room I overheard Mrs. Fuller saying, "Richard left a minute ago in a hurry. He said he'd miss the plane unless."

"That was the plan, Jane. He'll leave the car at the airport until he returns on Sunday night."

"How will you get back home?"

"We came in different cars. Richard didn't want me to give him a ride late at night and go back to pick him up late Sunday night."

"But still, he could have said goodbye before he packed off."

"I was actually looking for him. But Richard is Richard. That's the way he operates. I am accustomed to that."

"You are a very patient woman, Laura."

"I don't deny that."

"Richard is lucky to have you."

"That's for Richard to say."

*   *   *

"Sankar, you've got to do me a favor," Niles said.

I realized I had made a mistake coming into the yard again. I was about turn back when Niles grabbed my arm, hurting me.

"I did one for you when I faced that gorgon in the Financial Affairs office. It's your turn now."

He sounded very serious, almost threatening. I didn't want to tell him that I had gone to see Professor Czerny alone and that his contribution to my investigation was nil. I felt quite uneasy worried about being in his presence and worried, too, about his making a scene if I insisted on leaving.

"I don't have my car keys. I lost them or locked them in the car. Maybe I didn't even drive. That's it! Somebody drove me. Not my wife. She doesn't like parties. Stayed home doing creative writing. The stuff only English PhDs who read Henry James and James Joyce can understand. First class writing, so her friends say. I never understood that stuff. I'm a philippine - I mean philistine. You gotta read her works. Maybe you'll decipher it.... That's not what I wanted to talk about."

"The car keys."

"Oh, yes. You've got a memory like an elephant, Sankar... I've got to get home, right?"

"I can drop you off on our way."

"Good idea. But it won't work."

"Why?'

"Because I don't want to walk through that house. I don't want to be seen by anyone there."

I was at a loss and waited for him to come up with his own solution.

"I have an idea. A very good one. As good as your idea of shuffled cyanide bottles. See that gate in the wall. We go through that. That takes us into the alley. Then you and I walk to your car. You plop me in the car. That's the whole idea. Very clever. Eh?"

"What about my wife?"

"You go back and get her. I'll stay in the car until you come, thinking of cormorants and their sexy wives."

The yard was empty; the two sitting on the wall had gone in. Niles and I managed to get through the gate and into the dark alley unnoticed. Three hundred yards of rocky, unpaved ground lay between us and the street on which my Plymouth was parked. The alley, a thoroughfare for the Sanitary Engineering Department of the City of Gadsden, was bordered by walls and chain-link fences on one side and palo verde or creosote bushes on the other side. Beyond the trees and bushes lay an *arroyo*. I could hear the coyotes singing at some distance. We walked slowly, since I was afraid that one or both of us might trip over a rock and fall flat on his face. The moonlight made deep shadows making it difficult to walk on the uneven surface. I wondered and worried about what would happen, if we were to tumble down into the *arroyo* bottom or fall down in the alley. I was more worried about my being found in the company of a drunk than about my safety or Niles' safety. I asked Niles to walk behind me with his hands on my shoulder, while I moved slowly feeling the level of the ground as I slid my feet.

"I gotta take a leak," Niles said and angled toward the *arroyo*. I had a horrible thought of his falling on unfriendly desert plants or, worse yet, falling head-long into the wash.

I hurriedly redirected him toward the wall on the other side. He buttressed himself with a hand against the wall and let out a powerful stream. It took a very long time, or so it felt to me. The bladder must be the chief organ in his body in order to sustain that rate of delivery for such a long time, I thought. As Niles stayed supported by the wall, I looked back toward the Fullers' house for landmarks, since I would be coming back through the alley after depositing my drunken companion.

Some time later, I had Niles in the back seat of my Plymouth. I had parked the car on a side street at the end of the alley. Being the last to arrive, I had not been able to find a parking spot nearer to the Fullers' house.

Niles looked less exuberant than before.

"It may take a while to get Meera out of the party. I'll be back as soon as I can." I walked toward the alley.

"Sankar, come back" Niles called out.

Puzzled at the tone of his voice, I walked back to the car.

"Why are you going into that alley?"

"I want to get back to the party. Remember, Meera needs to go home too."

"Don't be stupid, Sankar. If you crawl through that alley at this time of the night, somebody is going to shoot you. Remember this is Gadsden city, center of the Wild West. Shoot first and think later. Guns, yes. Reason no."

I would have been mad at Niles, except for the sudden chill that invaded my bones.

*   *   *

"Sankar! I didn't see you go out," Jane Fuller greeted me as I quietly opened the front door and tried to slip into the living room unnoticed.

Even though she might have meant it as a casual remark, I felt as though I was caught red-handed during an illegal activity. "I walked around the neighborhood soaking up the moonlight and listening to the coyotes howling," I lied.

Well, I got an unexpected reaction. She said to the man next to her - another faculty member, I surmised - in an excited voice, "Did you hear what he said? Here we're wasting our time talking about faculty politics and who published what. And Sankar walks around enjoying nature and listening to coyotes!"

Jane Fuller elaborated on that theme. She and her husband had lost touch with nature, just like many Americans. Nobody in their neighborhood took time to enjoy the sight of cacti or the birds. Why was everybody rushing all the time, ignoring God's creation?

"He comes from an ancient civilization," the faculty member to whom I wasn't introduced said, "that lives in harmony with nature. We in the west, on the other hand, see nature as a menace, something to be controlled and subjugated."

Then he explained to Jane Fuller at length the changes in high school and college curriculum that should be made to develop the much needed sensitivity to nature in the students.

That was neither the first nor the last time I have been complimented for virtues I do not possess. I wandered away from the company looking for Meera.

*   *   *

If anyone ever gave honors for urban sprawl, Gadsden would be a strong contender for the first prize. Except for a few tall university and bank building, the town was covered with one-story houses or two-story apartment complexes that stretched twenty miles north-south and another twenty miles east-west. La Mariposa apartments to which I had to drive Niles were at the edge of the city, far away from the university area where we lived. As I drove, Niles babbled about many topics, but I couldn't follow anything he said. Towards the end of the journey he became decidedly silly again and started singing about one hundred bottles of beer on the wall.

When we reached our destination I stopped the car, got out, opened the back door and helped Niles out.

"Mrs. Sankar, here is an oriental riddle for you. What does an Indian say to his wife after the lights are out?" He asked as he got out of the car.

Meera didn't answer.

"He says, Sorry no sari. That's what he says. Sorry no…"

"Modern Indian women wear pajamas and not saris to bed." Meera said with the utmost seriousness.

I didn't know whether it was Meera's literal interpretation or Niles' enthusiasm for his own jokes that caused him to burst into a loud uproar. The consequences weren't good. A moment later he stumbled, and barely avoiding a prickly pear, fell into a bed of fairy dusters. By the time I managed to give him a hand, he had thrown up, covering himself and the plants with fowl smelling fluid.

I helped Niles to his apartment only to face an emaciated woman with thin lips and a very severe expression. "This isn't funny. Niles doesn't need friends like you egging him on to drink."

I tried to correct the wrong impression.

"He'll pay for it. Believe me, he will. You will too once I find out what went on at the party. And now good night."

The door slammed on my face. Well, I can't always expect to get compliments, I thought.

Chapter 14

Laws and Theories

Y ou really have a wonderful chairman," Bill Underwood said.

We were sitting in a corner of Professor Czerny's office then, in two comfortable chairs with an elegant coffee table between us.

I had come to work late, around one in the afternoon, reluctantly leaving home. I had stayed in bed till ten, exhausted by the previous night's partying. Since Zach had agreed to take Jay from his wilderness abode to school in the morning, I saw no reason to hurry.

Meera, once she realized that I was not going keep my usual schedule, started making *dosas*, potato-pea curry, *sambar* and coconut chutney. The little enthusiasm I had to go to the campus vanished as my nostrils were bombarded by the pungent and pleasant smells of Andhra cooking.

There was nothing I could do then about Gregg's case other than wait for the next committee meeting, even the thought of which made me feel very uncomfortable. I didn't want to interview more people and come up with a report that would please Professor Fuller. And I didn't have the resources to play the private eye to prove my theory. I had decided that I'd boldly propose my theory in the committee meeting whether Professor Fuller liked it or not. At least I could count on Niles taking my side. He owed me that much after what I had done for him the night before. Meanwhile I just had to get my mind off the case and jump into the lab work with both feet. Unfortunately I had zero momentum in that direction. Besides there was no point is starting the experiment that Friday, since I would be quitting in the middle of the afternoon to substitute for Professor Fuller in Chem 100.

I had walked into my office wondering how I could redirect my thinking from murder to molecules but, before I could sit at my desk and plan the day, Cathy Quintaro walked in saying, "Oh! Sankar! I'm glad you're here. Gregg's stepfather is downstairs. He came without an appointment. Could you please talk to him for a couple of minutes? Professor Czerny won't be in for another two hours and I can't find your boss anywhere."

Professor C was probably having a late lunch with some dean. My boss, Professor T, was probably stuffing his backpack with supplies for the weekend adventure since I'd be doing his discussion.

I walked into Professor Czerny's office to meet a stocky man dressed in shorts and a golf shirt. Cathy brought us coffee and cookies on a tray, after introductions.

"If I can do anything for you gentlemen, just holler," she said as she closed the door.

I felt like I was invited to give a seminar and my notes were snatched away from me before I could open my mouth. I didn't know what to say. Fortunately Bill Underwood took the initiative.

"We had the most enjoyable dinner with Dr. Czerny last night - my wife and I. Doris thinks very highly of him."

"Yes, he is doing a great job." What else could I have said?

"I understand there is a committee looking into issues raised by Gregg's suicide."

"Yes, we have just started." Issues? What a strange word!

"Dr. Czerny also mentioned that the faculty wants to start a scholarship fund - a memorial to Gregg."

Wonders are many but surprises are many more. "I haven't heard the details yet," was all I could say.

"Doris was excited. She'd do anything to beef up the fund."

I didn't know where the conversation was going. Not another committee, this time to raise money!

"She had already pledged twenty-five grand."

I searched for words and managed to say, "It's very generous."

"Not really. That's the least we can do."

I tried to visualize how Professor Czerny was able to convince the Underwoods to part with such a large sum to honor their not so distinguished son.

"You see Gregg was her only child."

Why was I being told all this?

"I knew Gregg's father. For a while we worked side by side at UPS. He was an extremely self-centered man with an alcohol problem. Very abusive on top of it. I think Gregg was about ten when Brad deserted Doris after cleaning the checkbook. She never heard from him after that. For all I know he's rotting in some jail."

I was getting curious. I said, "I didn't know anything about Gregg's father."

"Believe me, you don't want to know. When Doris and I tied the knot, I promised her that I'd be a good father to Gregg and I tried."

"It's very kind of you."

"I tried but Gregg had already crossed the line. You know what I mean?"

I wondered whether I should mention my assessment of Gregg's unpleasant nature, but kept quiet.

"By the time I had anything to do with Gregg he was already a big problem for Doris. They couldn't get along. It's like, if she says yes he has to say no. They couldn't stay in the same room without getting into a hissing match. More than once I had to come between the two to keep peace. It wasn't pleasant, I tell you. No, it was nasty and got worse with time. I never had the slightest trouble with my two daughters. They visit us frequently and Doris gets along with them wonderfully."

Why would a mother be concerned about scholarship fund for a son like Gregg? Why would the step-father put up with it?

"Well, things came to a closure last night, after dinner with your boss. We met him at La Posada del Bac. He picked up the tab, which I thought very decent of him. We barely got there on time from Phoenix. Oh, the food was heavenly. I don't know what the cook did for the mole sauce, it's the best I ever had. Getting back to Gregg, we had a heart to heart conversation with Professor C. After that, Doris and I saw for the first time why Gregg was like that. I understand he was doing first rate research. That shows Gregg was a very creative person. As Dr. Czerny said - and I read it in a magazine, too - creative people are hard to get along with. Einstein had a nasty temper when he was doing that relativity stuff. He wasn't the saint people saw later in life. Did you know that? Anyway the long and short of it is that Doris now knows what had been bothering Gregg. His mind was probably racing with ideas. As Professor C said, such people find life very frustrating and irritating."

Gregg and Einstein? I was too confused with the drift of the conversation to feel anything.

"When you think of it, it's not surprising Gregg killed himself. It gets so hard to be so far ahead of your colleagues and not be appreciated. Did you know that there were several cases of creative people committing suicide? It was a comfort to know for Doris. It's too bad Gregg killed himself before they had a couple of good hugs. At least she has some reason to feel happy about her son now."

Obviously some people are more useful to society after their death. I suppose I should have said something to add to Gregg's growing reputation, but I couldn't. Fortunately, Mr.

Underwood was not looking for corroboration and didn't mind, as far as I could tell from his demeanor, my being silent.

"I came here to deliver something and also to thank Professor Czerny, if he happened to be around. We are about to go back to Phoenix. We cleared the stuff from Gregg's apartment this morning. Gave most of it away to Junque for Jesus guys. After that we went to the bank. Doris knew that Gregg rented a safe deposit box to store the ring we gave him as a graduation gift. We thought we'd get this rigmarole about the will and a lawyer before they let's see what's in the box. We had absolutely no problem getting the stuff out of the box. People are very nice here. The bank manager checked the I.D. and presto we had the box on the table. The ring was there - a nice piece of jewelry. But we also found a research notebook with some pages marked important. Neither of us could make heads or tails out of it. It's Greek and Latin to us. I thought I'd show it to Dr. Czerny and ask his opinion."

"I am not sure about Dr. Czerny's calender," I said

"I came without checking his schedule. We can't stay in Gadsden anymore. We have to be in Phoenix by tomorrow. Doris has an important golf game. So I thought, what the heck I'll go and see whether the professor is in or not. If not, I knew I'd find somebody to talk to."

"Glad that I could be useful."

"This is what I think about the stuff in the notebook. I think they are like ideas for future research. A notebook full of plans. Whatever they are, they are no good to us. So I thought I'd drop the book here. I gave it to your lovely secretary. I understand you know something about what Gregg was doing. Maybe you can make some sense out of the stuff. I'd like to know what that's all about when you find out."

"Gregg was Professor Turner's student. I'll show the material to him."

"Maybe more than one person should go over the stuff. By the way, we got the copies of some pages notarized. The ones Gregg marked important. You know how it is. You have to be careful to protect what's yours. We don't want Gregg to lose the credit."

We parted with a firm handshake. Mr. Underwood's conversation left me jittery. Even though he was the one who talked all the time, without waiting for my reaction, I felt that it was I who had been telling lies. Why didn't I correct him and tell the truth about Gregg? Wouldn't it have been better to end this myth before it grew further?

This graduate student, whom I had barely known and who, after his death, had become very useful for professors in their devious plans and academic skirmishes, was controlling my mind. I felt that I must purge him from my thoughts or I'd go crazy. Fortunately, I had something else to worry about at that very moment - Dr. Turner's Chemistry 100.

As I was leaving Dr. Czerny's office, Cathy Quintaro offered the book to me.

"I think it should go to Professor Czerny," I said, hoping to disentangle myself for Gregg's life.

"He is not coming back today. If I leave the book here someone could easily steal it. People come and go into this office as they please. Hold on to it until you see the boss."

Reluctantly I accepted the book as if it were a corrosive chemical given to me for safekeeping.

The textbook for Professor Turner's course was titled *Chemistry: Fundamentals to Frontiers* and was written by four authors from four different universities. Under the title it was stated that the book was intended for a semester survey course for non-science students. But those were not the first things I noticed about the book. What caught my attention was the cover of the book, a picture of a rocket emitting a multicolored exhaust as it climbed to the zenith against a red tinted sky. And the unsuspected weight of the book, between two and three kilograms, almost made me drop it as my muscles strained.

The reason for the great bulk and density of the book - a book intended for a one-semester course - became clear once I started turning the pages. The figures and photos, that all but crowded out the text, were printed on a high-gloss clay paper. The art work was superbly rendered: even a mundane beaker became a dazzling object worthy enough to be held by the beautiful young woman who was in the process of pouring one colored liquid into another, while graciously looking away from the experiment to give you a winning smile.

Since the pages of the book reflected light at odd angles, I had to keep tilting it one way or the other to minimize the glare while trying to read the text. The first chapter was an essay on various ills that plague our life on the planet earth - from cancer to pollution - and how chemistry could abolish them in due course. I didn't think Professor Turner would cover that chapter. The second chapter was titled "The Tools of Science" and reviewed basic math - such as the multiplication of decimal numbers and the use of scientific notation in writing numbers. I knew I could handle any questions on that matter and skipped the entire chapter. If I had more time I would have read the text of the separate interviews with Professors Clara Millbright and Jauquin Lopez-Perez - two distinguished chemistry professors who, the blurb claimed, use mathematics extensively in their research. The interviews were printed in their entirety along with very becoming photographs of the two scientists. I had never heard about either of them before.

The next chapter was about the scientific method: data acquisition, hypotheses, laws and theories. From what I knew about Professor Turner's attitude on non-technical discussion of science, I could safely say that he would never be caught lecturing on the material of that chapter. The fourth chapter introduced the ideas of matter, atoms and molecules and I remembered that this was where Professor Turner had said he had begun the course. I tried to read the chapter but I couldn't see any step-by-step development of the ideas. Boxed articles on the smallness of the atom, the magnification needed to make it the size of a baseball and other such matters broke up the main text in the middle of sentences. Then there were other boxes devoted to biographies of eminent scientists like Avogadro and Dalton, and to a qualitative discussion of recently built microscopes that could actually see atoms. Then came the photographs of what appeared to be undulating landscapes but turned out to be computer-enhanced pictures of atoms. After a few minutes of browsing I decided that I would not be able to read the chapter, within the allotted time, and discover the pedagogical approach used by the authors. I would answer the questions from my general knowledge and not worry about referring the students to the relevant pages in the book.

Professor Turner wasn't off the mark when he said that no more than ten out of the two hundred registered students would be in the first discussion class. I counted twelve students scattered over the big hall as I hurried into the class room. At least the number of students attending was appropriate for a discussion period.

I was a few minutes late. I would have been on time or even ahead, except for an unexpected twist at the last minute. As I finished examining the book I noticed that I had at least ten minutes before the class started. I was telling myself that this would be more than adequate time to saunter from my room to any corner of the building when an uneasy thought had crossed my mind. Where did the class meet? I had rushed to the main office and inquired.

"FEM 408."

"What is FEM?"

"Free Enterprise and Marketing building."

That building was almost a mile away at the other end of the campus. I jumped on my bike and pedaled as fast as I could. I should have realized, I blamed myself as I hurried, how the class rooms were scattered in our research-one campus. Many student labs had been converted into research labs and lecture rooms, into research or business offices. The few rooms available for instruction were scattered across the campus and used continuously. Thus tutorials, special seminars and discussions have to be conducted in less-used rooms on the periphery of the campus.

I was panting, from strenuous bicycling and running up the stair well, as I hurried along the aisle to the blackboard. I didn't think I would be able to speak coherently for a few minutes, so I turned to the blackboard and, while catching my breath, wrote in big letters: "Chemistry 100. Professor Franklin Turner's Discussion Period."

After a pause I wrote: "Sankar" in a separate line and "Understudy to Professor Turner" on a line below that and quietly appreciated my own ready wit.

By that time my heart had reached its normal rhythm and I was ready to address the class. I turned toward the students and said, "Now that the introduction is complete are there any questions?"

Two students got up and walked out of the room. One of them turned back and asked, "Say Doc, wouldya know where Nootrition 101 meets?"

I said no and wondered how many of Professor Turner's students were frantically looking for the right classroom at that very moment. After all it was the first week of a new semester and such confusion was probably not uncommon on a huge campus where class descriptions didn't match the building names.

A student in the third row raised his hand and began saying, "Dr. Understudy, do you ..."

So much for my sense of humor!

"I am not Dr. Understudy. I'm Dr. Sankar." I turned to the blackboard and underlined my name. As I was doing that another student got up and left.

The fellow who had started to ask a question shrugged his shoulder and said, "Doc, do you know if Professor Turner grades on a curve?"

"You should ask Professor Turner that question."

"Yes, he grades on a curve," said a student sitting right in the middle of the room. He wore a white shirt and a tie - unusual attire for a student - and looked supremely confident.

That seemed to have exhausted the topics of discussion momentarily. I scanned the faces in the scantily occupied class room. A girl in a miniskirt and micro top sat in the first row swinging her legs rhythmically. She smiled vaguely in my direction.

"When is the first exam?" The question came from the back of the room.

"Professor Turner hasn't told me." Weren't there any questions I could answer?

"The first exam is on February 24 Wednesday. Covers chapters four through seven." The fellow in the white shirt said looking into his assignment book.

"Law and theory. I don't know," the oriental student sitting in the corner said while shaking his head.

I took it as a request for an explanation of how laws and theories are distinguished. I wished I had been fielded a technical question, something about structure of atoms or the mole concept.

Most elementary textbooks of chemistry start with exalting words about the scientific method and how laws are discovered and theories forged. Yet I know of no professor who takes this chatter with any seriousness or devotes any classroom time to the material.

However, not wanting to brush the question aside, I said, "Briefly stated laws are rules by which nature functions and theories are our constructs to explain those laws." I tried to elaborate on that theme but I was rudely interrupted by a large woman with a sharp voice.

"I took this course before at Greenlee Junior College. I really know my stuff. But I have to take the course again here since this damn university won't allow transfer credit for a course with even a C plus grade. We had an excellent professor there, a genius who worked with what's his name who got the Nobel Prize in geography. He told us that laws are always right and theories are only sometimes right. That makes perfect sense to me. And what you're saying is very confusing."

Well, I heard even a better one. Laws are what we don't understand; theories are what we cannot explain. But how could I defend myself against this intense woman who was convinced that information she received at Greenlee was superior to what I was giving at Gadsden? I didn't have to since the know-it-all in the white shirt joined with the comments:

"The definitions for law and theory are given in section three-four. Professor Turner said we could omit that section."

The discussion came to an end. I noticed that the oriental student, who had asked the question, was busily reading his book. The mini-skirted, micro-topped girl in front was still swaying her legs, vaguely looking in my direction with a smile.

A few minutes of uneasy silence passed during which the woman from the Greenlee School of Philosophy of Science got up and left. It was clear that there would be no questions regarding the subject. So I suggested that anyone with questions on the assigned problems should come to the front and then added, "I'd like to talk to anyone who knew Gregg Westover."

Gregg, as a teaching assistant, might have been in contact with some of the students in undergraduate courses. Nevertheless I wondered why I had said that. Would Gregg's ghost haunt me forever?

The oriental student came to the bench. He said, "You ex-explain law and theory. One hundred per cent correct." He left with a bow.

The woman in the miniskirt came up next and, leaning forward on the table and lifting her eyes to me, said, "I'm Brenda." She said it as though I should have known her.

"Hi."

"You wanted to see me .. about Gregg."

"You knew him?"

"I was dating the jerk for a while. We broke up, ah, about three months ago."

"What was he like."

"Pretty mean, he was always mad at somebody or other."

"Did he specifically mention any names?"

"He hated everybody."

"Did he say anything about a particular professor?"

"Maybe. I don't remember."

"Did he say why?"

"I don't think he needed a reason. He just hated people."

"Is that why you broke up?"

"Not just that. He tried to use me."

"Use you?" Vague images of thoroughly despicable behavior floated in my mind.

"Yeah"

"What do you mean?"

"There was this workshop - for guys who want to start a business. You get loans and stuff like that. Gregg wanted me to go with him and pretend I was his fiancée."

"Why?"

"He said, 'to impress the suits.' He said they'd trust him if he was about to be married and settle down."

"Did you go?"

"I did. At the workshop he was all nice to me. He could be a charmer, if he wanted. But I am not stupid. I could see through the guy. He was putting up a show for the big guys. When it was all over he acted as though I was a piece of ... you know..."

"Did he get a loan?" I wondered whether that was the source of money Gregg had mentioned to Martha Gwinn.

"No. The guys running the show knew their stuff. You think they're going to be taken in by a sleaze ball like Gregg? Then Gregg was mad at me 'cause it was all my fault. So he said. So I said to myself, 'Hey, Brenda! What are you doing with this guy? He's going to screw you and then drive you into the nut house. Get rid of him, girl!' So we broke up."

I was trying to picture Gregg's behavior when Brenda said, "And another thing. Gregg did mean things. Not that he had to, you know. Not like he was pushed against a wall and stuff like that. He just had to be mean."

I asked Brenda to give me an example. She remained thoughtful before answering.

"One of my friends - she's from California. She copied data ... from a friend's notebook. It's not that she was cheating or anything like that. She didn't have any time that week for the lab report. She was going to repeat the whole course anyway, you know, and learn the stuff. Not just for the grade but really to understand it. Gregg was her TA and found out. He wanted her to pay him five hundred bucks. Otherwise he was going to fail her or report her to the dean. And she didn't have the money. She didn't want her mom to know either. It was pretty traumatic."

"What did she do?"

"She withdrew from the U. You can do that, but you have to drop all the courses. Withdraw totally. She told her mom that she was sick and stuff like that."

"Why didn't she go to the dean?"

"She didn't want her mom to find out. Gregg had the lab reports with him and she was afraid he would tell her mom."

"When did this happen?"

"Last Spring. But I found out only last month, after Gregg and I stopped dating. Bonnie called from Denver and this came up in the conversation. She's really happy now. She's married and has a job with a bank and a nice apartment and stuff like that. She and her mom get along fine now."

"When did you last see Gregg?"

"Oh, I used to see him everyday."

"I thought you stopped dating."

"Yep! That's over. Thank God. He lives, I mean, lived in the apartment right opposite from me. It's a very big apartment complex with swimming pools between the buildings. So I'd see Gregg going and coming. I never said a word to him after we broke up."

I was quick to realize that I had, in front of me, a possible witness to Gregg's movements during the days before the murder.

"Have you noticed anything unusual going on during the last week or the previous weeks? Any visitors?"

"I was gone most of the Christmas break. Visiting grandma in Kansas. She's ninety years old and remembers everything. The day I came back – that was Tuesday last week, nine days back – I saw a good-looking woman and Gregg arguing. In front of his apartment. I had the full view. But I didn't think anything of it. Gregg was always quarreling with the neighbors. About noise, parking space and stuff like that. Then this woman comes back in the afternoon as I was taking a load to the laundry. They started arguing again in front of the pool."

Gregg was killed on Saturday, four days later. Is there a connection between that quarrel in the apartment complex area and murder in chemistry building?

"Any idea what they were arguing about?"

"They were at it when I came back from the laundry room. I didn't want to get too close to them. I didn't want to be anywhere near that jerk. So I didn't hear all the stuff going between them.

"Do you know anything about this woman? Does she live in that apartment complex?"

"No. I don't know where she lives. She drove a red beamer. I am sure about it."

"Do you, by any chance, remember the license plate number?

"I probably wrote it down."

Brenda opened her University of Gadsden Semester Planner and flipped the pages.

"Here it is. R38 SC2"

I thanked her while I jotted down the number.

"I feel sorry for him though," Brenda said as she was leaving. "He didn't have to kill himself. There is so much help out there."

I asked her why she thought Gregg killed himself.

"Why do I think he killed himself? Because he didn't have God's peace. If you don't have God's peace you are always angry. One day you'll kill yourself. I know that because I went through anger therapy for three years before I could straighten myself out. It's scary, what anger does to you. Now that I've found God's peace I'm not angry at any one. I tried to teach that to Gregg, but he wouldn't listen."

If there is one thing that continues to puzzle me in my adopted country, it is the invocation of God under unexpected circumstances, very much like the appearance of the symbol for the prince of peace, I could not help noticing, dangling in the valley between Brenda's partially exposed mounds of pneumatic bliss. Perhaps I am betraying my narrow-minded provincialism whenever I am surprised to hear God's name outside the chants of holy men or the murmuring prayers of women with covered heads. Why shouldn't a sensuously dressed young woman, talking about anger - and stuff like that - have as much right to God's name as any who abandon this world for His company?

"I was out of control, wasn't I?" Niles said across the table in the student union.

"You said it."

After my failed attempt to educate Chem 100 class, I returned to the Chemistry building to collect my things and go home for the weekend. I wasn't expecting to be delayed by Niles Baxter who looked worse for wear with blood-shot eyes and crumpled clothes.

"It's not just one thing, Sankar. I'm getting hit from all directions."

"Sorry to hear that."

"Yesterday afternoon as I was getting ready for the party I got a call from one of my colleagues. He said that my thesis advisor at UC, Chuck Randolph, didn't get tenure. That shook me up."

"You must admire him to take it personally."

"I do, Sankar. I do. He's a first rate scientist. He should've been promoted. But there's more to his not getting tenure. It throws a dark shadow on my future."

"How is that?"

"My chance of getting tenure down the road is zero."

"I don't see the connection."

"Randolph didn't get tenure because he couldn't raise money. That means no body thought his work is important. If I continue to work in the area that I did my Ph. D., I will be no better shape than Randolph. It'd be just impossible to get a grant. Ergo no tenure."

"Can't you change your direction?"

"Not practical. This is my second year here. I have to produce the results within the next three years to hold on to my job. Not just publications. I have to show the administrator that I can raise big money too."

Even though it was Niles' problem, I felt it personally. If I ever could start as an assistant professor in some university, I'd be in the same boat as Niles. Neither my thesis advisor nor any of the other professors I worked with were members of influential committees with capacities to spread research dollars around. Thus it might not be easy to get funding even if I had a brilliant idea. But the sad fact was I didn't have any earth-shattering ideas. I believed that I had been a competent researcher with an occasional clever idea. I also believed that what I had been doing was useful research for the development of science as a whole. I wondered: Isn't there a place in this country of bounty for someone like me?

Comparing my troubles with Niles', however, was like comparing apples and pears. He already had a faculty position and he could possibly move to a university with less emphasis on research. Besides he was younger than me and, being childless, freer to take risks.

"There ought to be something you can do," I said.

"Yes. I could take a study leave, go to work with somebody well-known."

"You could even look for a better position from there."

"Unfortunately that's not for me."

"Why?"

"Philippa will not cooperate. She says her creative writing will suffer if we move from here. She doesn't want me to go by myself for a year or even a semester. Too much crime in Gadsden for her to stay alone – that's what she says."

I didn't know what advice, if any, I could offer, or whether I was expected to give any. When it comes to personal relations in this culture I am truly a foreigner.

"When I think how helpful Laura has been for Richard's career I feel very jealous. Yes, I don't mind admitting it. My wife, unfortunately, turned out to be a burden on me."

"Richard's lucky"

"You can say that again. I don't think he'd have gotten as far as he did without Laura running errands and coordinating everything."

"That's for sure."

"Sankar, I don't mind saying it to you. But I am sure Richard's a real scoundrel. He doesn't appreciate what he has. Not an atom of decency in him. He is incapable of loving anyone beyond himself. I think he's just using Laura to further his own career."

Niles realized that I was feeling uncomfortable with the drift of the conversation.

"I'm sorry, Sankar, to be so negative. But I don't have a good feeling about people like Richard Blackwell."

There wasn't anything I could have said then without sounding either nosy or patronizing. Fortunately Niles ended the conversation by saying, "Thanks for listening. I needed to talk to someone like you"

*   *   *

"So you want me to find out who the mystery woman was," Zach said.

I had called Zach after I got home and told him about my conversation with Brenda in Professor Fuller's discussion section.

"I don't know."

"What don't you know?"

"I don't think I should waste more time playing a detective. I should get back to my research."

"So you are not curious who this woman was?"

"I didn't say that, Zach. I am afraid of losing more time."

"Perhaps. But you can't give up in the middle. That isn't allowed."

"Who says?"

"I says. You will know her identity by Monday. I promise you that."

"Zach, she might not have anything to do with this case."

"Facts first, my friend. Get back to your research while I do my research."

Chapter 15

A Couple of Suspects

I don't see anything here," I said while examining the lab notebook Bill Underwood had brought to the chemistry department. I was sitting at our tiny dining table having my breakfast.

"That is because your plate is empty. Another *idli*?"

Meera knew perfectly well that my comments were about the pages in the book and not about the empty plate in front of me. Over years we developed the habit of deliberate misunderstanding of each other on things that didn't matter and then carry on illogical debate. I don't know what the marriage counseling theorists think of bantering about inconsequential things as a method of communication, but it seems to work for us. I should have said something like: "Your *idlis* are making me blind."

Instead I kept quiet while examining the pages. Meera got the message that I wasn't in a mood to banter and said, "What were you expecting?"

"I'll tell you in a minute."

I must admit that as Bill Underwood was portraying Gregg as an obsessive and devoted scientist (based on the information imparted to him by Professor Czerny), I had had a hard time keeping a straight face. Nevertheless I was able to control myself and attend to my duties as a sympathetic listener with utmost seriousness. I had brought home the notebook, and the articles from Gregg's desk, in my backpack only with the intention of keeping them safe in my possession until I could turn them over to Professor Czerny personally. I had no interest in opening the notebook to find out what was in it.

As I was getting up this morning, however, I wondered whether there was some possibility that Gregg was indeed a visionary of big ideas in science and whether my premature judgment was unwarranted. I knew Gregg was not a good student and that he had been mean to others. But where was it written that such a person might not be a leader in science? In fact I could name a few first rate scientists who were no better than Gregg in their attitudes and who also showed no promise during their school days.

Once such doubts arose in my head, I could not resist opening the notebook to see what was in it. My first surprise was to discover that the notebook wasn't Gregg's. It belonged to Professor Blackwell, who kept neat and meticulous records of his laboratory work for the year 1987. I wondered how Gregg got hold of that notebook since scientists – particularly Professor Blackwell's type – tend to be very possessive of their records. I knew Gregg was a graduate student in Professor Blackwell's laboratory during 1991-92. Did the professor assign a problem to Gregg that needed the information in that notebook? In that case Gregg should have returned the book when he changed research advisors. Instead, he kept it in a safe deposit box as if it were a valuable treasure. Why?

While keeping my questions about the possession of the notebook in suspense, I leafed through the pages, particularly the pages with stickums and notes scribbled on them. I couldn't find anything special about them. There were tables with numbers and subtitles on top of each column. The investigations were about fluorescence, a glow compounds show when illuminated by light.

The names of the compounds, for which these data were collected, were clearly marked on the top of the pages. The page following the tables had references to synthetic procedures used in preparing the compounds. Other than the results of a routine investigation there was nothing unusual.

I explained to Meera why I said I didn't see anything earlier. She leaned over and looked at the pages as she dropped an *idli* on my plate.

"What are those strange symbols on the stickums?" Meera asked.

"Greek letters," I had not paid attention to them before.

"But what do they say?'

The symbols that puzzled Meera read φραυδ. It took me a while to realize that the Greek letters did not denote abstract mathematical entities, as thy usually did in scientific work. Instead, they formed the word "fraud" written with the Greek alphabet. I took the book to my desk in the bedroom and examined the rest of the marked pages. And I went over the heavily marked articles by Professor Blackwell I had found in Gregg's desk on Thursday. It soon became clear that the data Professor Blackwell had published were not what he had recorded in his notebook. I wondered why he did that. I couldn't find any reason for reporting the wrong data. Equally puzzling was the question: How did Gregg find out about the discrepancy?

"The two articles with cooked-up data were published in 1988, the year Blackwell interviewed for a faculty appointment at the university," I said to Meera. I had just returned from the university library after reading several articles published earlier by Professor Blackwell. "The year before that he published a theory predicting the fluorescence properties of molecules. The experiments did not agree with his theory and so he made up the data that supports his theory."

"He can do that? Don't they check the data before publishing?"

"If you mean the editors or reviewers, the answer is simply they can't check the accuracy of the data. They will take the author's words if the procedures used were documented."

"If other researchers repeat the experiments you could get into trouble."

"That happens only if somebody thinks the experiments are important. That's the only time the results get checked. What I think happened was that Blackwell published a theory and no one paid attention to it. I couldn't find any citations for that theory except in his two papers. I think he dashed off those articles with fake data to impress the search committee and improve his chances of getting a job. It just added two more papers to his long list of publications. He didn't expect that anyone would even care to read them."

"How did Gregg find out?"

"I don't know. Somehow he stumbled on those articles."

"Was he blackmailing Professor Blackwell?"

"Possibly."

It was time to drive Jay to a soccer game. I took the book and papers with me as I rushed to the car with Jay.

*   *   *

As the soccer match was going on, with parents showing more enthusiasm than their boys and frequently yelling at the top of their lungs, I could not stop thinking about my earlier find. It was quite likely that Gregg tried to blackmail Professor Blackwell. He had been practicing the art of blackmail for years. But I couldn't see him succeeding with Blackwell. There were several ways the professor could easily defend himself against the charges of fraud. These articles were not significant for his reputation as a productive scientist. They were minor excursions into backwaters. Besides the data he published could have been recorded in another book. It would be hard to prove that he deliberately cheated, even if he had done so. Since the publication of those articles he had established himself as a very successful grant-getter. It's unlikely that a university would do anything other than turn a blind eye when it comes to faculty with big grants, unless there is a hue and cry from a large segment of the scientific community. No one in administration would pay attention to the ranting of a dishonest graduate student like Gregg or investigate a researcher like Professor Blackwell with big grants.

I couldn't see Blackwell taking it as a serious threat, if Gregg had in fact approached him for blackmail payment. I certainly couldn't see his taking the risk of poisoning Gregg when he could be easily discredited.

While I was still occupied with the above thoughts, Jay's team won by a single point and a great jubilation followed the victory, with parents giving the team accolades suitable for those who had successfully scaled Mt. Everest. When we reached home after an ice cream break, I left the notebook in the car without thinking. That turned out to be a serious mistake on my part.

*   *   *

"You are going to be surprised," Meera said as I returned from a walk. It was probably around nine thirty in the evening. I had played a couple of games of chess with Jay before going out to do a two mile loop in my usual slow pace.

"Surprised about what?"

"That is what Zach said. He called ten minutes back and wanted to talk to you. I said you are walking. Zach said, 'I want to surprise him. Can I come now?' I said why drive all the way so late in the night. He said, 'Because I want to surprise your man.' I said, it is his townhouse, we are not even paying the full rent and he can come every time he wanted. He said 'he will not come if we don't like it'."

I suspected that Meera summarized what was probably an involved conversation in which she tried unsuccessfully to find the nature of the surprise, while encouraging Zach to visit us.

"Is Zach coming or not?"

"He is coming."

*   *   *

"Three guesses! Who owns the red beamer?" Zach asked me as he walked into the living room.

It was nearly ten, close to my usual bed time. Meera came down to greet Zach dressed in pajamas and a robe.

"I'll make coffee unless you want tea."

Zach knew it would be futile trying to prevent Meera from playing hostess.

"Decaf please ... and no sweets." Give in a bit and then draw a line. Zach knew how to deal with Meera.

"So what's your guess?" Zach asked again.

"I am drawing a blank"

"What sort of detective are you?"

"Not a good one obviously. Never claimed to be one."

"So you give up."

"Yes. I don't have a clue. Tell me." It was late for me to think straight.

"The car with the license plate R38 SC2 is registered to Professor Richard Blackwell of the chemistry department."

I didn't know whether I was surprised or not. Ever since I talked to Professor Blackwell on Tuesday I had been suspecting bad blood between him and Gregg. My suspicion was confirmed by Blackwell's attitude at the party and what Brenda had told me the previous day, at the end of the class. She had said that Gregg had an intense dislike for Professor Blackwell and the people in his pod. If the car spotted in front of Gregg's apartment belonged to Professor Blackwell, the woman seen with Gregg was very likely Laura Blackwell. How does she fit into the picture? An affair – between Laura and one of her husband's previous students?

"How did you find out?" I asked as my brain was trying to connect the dots.

"I have friends in high places."

Zach knew someone in the university police department. It took Zach a few hours to reach him at home, but after that it was a matter of minutes to pull the name out of the files.

"It wouldn't have been that easy, if the car didn't have a university sticker."

Meera joined us with coffee cups.

"So who killed Gregg?" Zach raised the question. "I thought that's the burning question and not the car registration."

After days of nothing to go by, I found a lead this morning when I examined Professor Blackwell's notebook for the year 1987. Now there was another lead, thanks to Zach. They were not pointing in the same direction.

"Lost in your thoughts?" Zach said.

"I suppose so. There's something else you should know."

I told Zach about the notebook.

"So both Richard and Laura might be involved in the murder."

"Looks that way."

"But you don't think Gregg was blackmailing the professor."

"He might have tried, but his case is weak."

"You may think that way. But Blackwell could see it differently."

"Who is going to believe Gregg's word against big fund raiser like Blackwell?"

"It's not a question of belief. Once the word got around, other researchers might repeat the experiment and show that Blackwell's a fraud."

"Zach, people repeat experiments only if they think they are important. Blackwell faked the data to bolster a theory that no one takes seriously. He was just padding his publication list. Scientists are not going to get into a fray unless they get something out of it other than proving someone else wrong."

"You have a point there. But you can't rule out Blackwell being the agent of death. What if those two papers are just a tip of the iceberg? In that case Blackwell would certainly take even the slightest hint regarding his lack of integrity seriously. His whole career might come tumbling down, if he yields to Gregg."

"There is another possibility," Meera said as she pushed a plate of *mysore pak* toward Zach.

"Meera, I said no sweets."

"The coffee is not very good. You need something sweet to go along with coffee."

"The coffee is fine, just fine."

"Coffee tastes better with *mysore pak*."

"Meera, what is the other possibility?" I wanted the conversation move past *mysore pak*.

"Laura Blackwell said tenure decision is held back by the provost."

"So it's the wrong time to be blackmailed," Zach said.

"OK. We will agree that Richard Blackwell had a strong motive and he could have poisoned Gregg."

"Means, motive and opportunity – all there," Zach said,

I wasn't pleased with the conclusion. Not that I felt any sympathy for Professor Blackwell. I just remembered my role in the committee. How should I present the information I had? Should I just give them the notebook and leave it at that? I might have been contented doing that before I ever looked into the pages of the notebook. Now I felt lost.

"Where does Laura Blackwell come in?" Zach raised the question.

"I am not sure, but she might not know anything about the faked data," I said.

"How can you be certain?"

"Even though she was a constant companion in the lab, she did not have a science background. And Richard Blackwell would not voluntarily tell her what was going on."

"We may be looking at another motive here," Zach said.

"What would that be?"

"One of the oldest. She was having an affair with Gregg. Perhaps Richard Blackwell got a whiff of it and decided to remove the competition."

"Impossible. Very, very impossible, Zach." Meera was quick to announce.

"Why?"

"Laura is a very dutiful wife."

I wondered whether we were about to hear another lecture on inalienable duties.

"I don't know much about dutiful wives, Meera. But I know that when a married woman gets into an affair it isn't because she doesn't know her duties. It's a desperate attempt to get some affection. I bet Laura is starved for affection, living with Blackwell."

Meera didn't come up with a counter argument but shook her head to indicate that she didn't agree with Zach.

I too had difficulty accepting Zach's idea.

"There is a flaw in your argument, Zach. I agree that Blackwell is a very self centered person. Why would such a person go to the extreme, if his wife wanders off? You'd think he would forget her and look for some other bed partner and servant."

"You guys need a course in human nature. She talks about duties. And you think that people act without emotions. Blackwell may not care for his wife. He may ignore her for his career or treat her like a doormat. But if somebody gets into her bed that's a different matter. It's like somebody stole his property. Revenge is the answer. The only answer."

I was aware of the mild insults Zach was dishing out. I ignored them as I tried to grapple with my own thoughts.

It appeared to me, as I thought about the problem of man, woman and the *tertium quid* - as Kipling called the third in a triangle – that uneducated men in predominantly agricultural societies generally considered women as their property, like an ancestral home or land on which generations of the same family farmed. In normal times the men folk respect and defend their women in the same way they value and defend their ancestral property. In case of conflict the women are raped by enemies in the spirit of marauding victors spreading destruction through the vanquished lands. I had no difficulty imagining intense jealousies, murdering hatreds arising from even inconsequential encounters between a married woman and a bachelor in such societies. Educated men in developed countries, I felt, treated women as companions and friends. In such a culture, one could be very disappointed in an unfaithful companion but the reaction would never be as intense as when one has lost forever the ancestral home.

It took me a while to explain my theory to Zach.

"Interesting theory. But I don't agree with you," he said finally.

"What don't you agree with?"

"I don't think there is any difference between cultures on a gut level. Your average peasant may think of his wife as landed property, but people like Richard Blackwell think of their wives as stock in a company. They'd be no less brutal in protecting their property."

I was surprised that Zach had come up with such a thesis.

"Your peasant would never let go of his property," Zach continued, "but modern man is always worried about depreciation and is always looking for a better stock."

"I suppose your perspective may be different than that of a married man." That was a cagey remark on my part. I had been curious to find out whether Zach had ever been married and since he wasn't in the habit of divulging the details of his personal life, I thought I'd take this occasion to pry into his past.

"I've been married and divorced - married for three years. But that's got nothing to do with what we're talking about."

I'd have liked to ask him about his married life and whether he and his former wife had any children, but I knew Zach would not answer. Why was he so reluctant to talk about himself and his past?

Indeed Zach changed the topic as if to prevent me from coming up with questions about his past life.

"When I was a grad student," he said, "I used to hear this about one of the profs at a mega-university. The old geezer was from somewhere in Eastern Europe. Just when everyone's convinced that he would live and die a bachelor, he surprises them by marrying an attractive woman thirty-five years his junior. Of course, he doesn't pay her any attention after the wedding, being absorbed in his own research. After a couple of years the wife gets disgusted and elopes with one of his talented grad students. A few years go by and the romance between the grad student and the young wife turns sour. The student then returns to the university and goes to see the old man in his crowded office, busily scribbling something or other on the papers scattered over the desk. Once he gets the old prof's attention he asks him whether he could continue on the project he had left unfinished when he ran away with the man's wife. The old codger gives him a piercing look for thirty seconds over the rims of the glasses hanging on his nose, chuckles to himself and says, 'Why not? After all a good graduate student is hard to find. A bad wife? Easy. Very easy.'"

"You made it up. Didn't you?"

"Doesn't matter. Maybe if Gregg had been a good student, Richard Blackwell would have accepted the situation." Zach got up and helped himself to another cup of coffee. He poured some into Meera's cup.

"I didn't want any more, Zach."

"Fair is fair. You keep pushing food on me and I should have the same privilege."

"I am not sure how I am going to bring all this up in the committee."

"We are not done yet, Sankar. There's another suspect."

"Who?"

"Laura Blackwell."

"I am telling you Laura is a very good person," Meera said.

"Meera, we have to consider all possibilities until we zero in on the killer," Zach said in a conciliatory tone.

"So why are you not considering the possibility that Laura is a good person?"

Obviously she didn't expect the answer, since she moved away into the kitchen.

"Laura has the means. She knows the layout of the chemistry building. Gregg would have accepted the cyanide doped soda without an iota of suspicion, if Laura gave it to him." Zach said.

I remembered the conversation at the party. Laura had claimed that she knew more about Blackwell's lab than he did. Undoubtedly she had access to all the keys and chemicals. As Zach said, she could have poisoned Gregg more easily than Richard. But why?

"Let's say she's having an affair with the scum ball Gregg. Best way to suppress the news before her husband finds out was to get rid of the lover," Zach said.

"So she is also a suspect."

"That' right. Both Richard and Laura have means, motives and opportunities to get rid of Gregg."

They had the means, motives and opportunity to whisk off the cyanide bottle from the lab in the nick of time. I was now convinced that one of them had learned about my search through the orders for chemicals from Professor Czerny.

"So which of the two did it?" I asked.

"That's for you to find out."

If an affair was at the root of the crime, either of them might have done it: Richard out of jealousy and Laura for concealing it. Richard was the likely killer if Gregg had tried blackmail.

"Things still don't add up in my mind," I said.

"Give it some rest. Get a good night's sleep. You will see better tomorrow," Zach said as he got up to leave

It was past eleven. The last few days had been strenuous. I should have agreed to Zach's suggestion and gone to bed. Instead I made the fatal mistake of raising a question which inspired Zach to come up with a plan. It almost killed us.

Chapter 16

The Lady with a Gun

Z ach, we overlooked something very important."
"What was that?" Zach asked as he was leaving.

"The university registers cars in Fall. This is the
beginning of the Spring semester. The Blackwell's might have
sold that BMW."

Gadsden was built for the automobile age. There were at
least as many functioning cars in the city as there were people. If
you also count the derelicts people keep in their yards, with the
hopes of making classics out of corpses, you get a much larger
number. The major obsession for the residents seemed to be
buying and selling cars which they kept, on the average, for three
years. On any given day, a fourth or more of the residents would
be shopping for cars or trucks. About eighty per cent of the
advertisement space in the two dailies was devoted to automobile
commerce. Even if the Blackwells weren't as devoted to cars as
the citizens of Gadsden, it wasn't completely unlikely that they
had sold the car for a more recent model.

"In that case Richard would have registered the new car,
unless he wants to pay for both old and new. Don't you know
what university parking permits cost?"

Yes, I knew. At three hundred and fifty dollar a parking permit, I could not afford even the cheapest. A thousand dollars and above for a reserved space, such as the one Professor Czerny holds on to, was way beyond my means.

"You're probably right, Zach. Very likely the Blackwells still own the BMW." I was tired and ready for bed.

Zach changed his mind. He said, "The records might not be up to date. If the car was sold over the Christmas break, it might still be listed under Blackwell's name."

"I suppose you can find out tomorrow or Monday by calling your friend at the parking services," I said. I felt distressed that the investigation, which I thought had come to a conclusion of a sort, was about to begin again.

"There is an easier way."

"Easy or difficult, it has to wait for another day, Zach. I am falling asleep on my feet."

"Get up. We are going to drive past Blackwell's house," Zach said decisively as he looked up their address in the phone book.

"It's almost midnight, Zach," I pleaded.

"No time to waste then."

*   *   *

We didn't leave right away. We had to wait for another twenty-seven minutes.

"Why?" Zach asked when Meera told us that we must wait.

Meera offered no explanation but went ahead to block the door. Zach looked puzzled. I knew the answer but didn't want to divulge. As Zach was pushing me to get ready to go, Meera had gone up to consult the esoteric astrological calendar published by Venkateswarulu and Co, Spice and Sweetmeat Merchants, Vijayawada, A. P. for free distribution. Meera had decided the auspicious time for our adventure and there could be no argument about it. She would stay in front of the door until that moment.

*   *   *

"They live in the foothills, as you might have guessed," Zach said as he started the car again. "6372 Camino Santiago. I know the guys who designed homes in that neighborhood."

I am wary of unfamiliar neighborhoods. I wouldn't casually wander into one even in the daytime let alone in the middle of the night.

"Zach, it's almost one in the morning. Can't we do it tomorrow, when we can see the mailboxes?"

"You're the one who wanted to know whether the Blackwells still own that BMW. Let's find out. It will only take fifteen minutes."

"Probably five minutes the way you drive."

I was wrong. Zach drove my car very slowly, once we were in the suburbs, frequently switching the head lights between high and low. We left his truck behind since it was low on gas.

"This is not an interstate," Zach said. "You have a lot of night life in the outskirts. Coyotes, javelina, cottontails and domestic animals that don't know any better. You should be prepared to stop on a dime."

Once we got into the subdivision we had to slow down even more. The driver's view was restricted to a car length or two by the narrow sinuous road that suddenly dipped and doubled back as it crossed a wash between hills. The street signs at the intersections of meandering roads were hidden by overgrown mesquite and palo verde. It took nearly thirty minutes before we spotted the Blackwells' house, which was set back more than fifty feet from an abrupt bend in the road. The house was partly concealed from the road by ocotillo and creosote bushes. The carport, with its gaping entrance perpendicular to the front wall of the house, was at one side of the long house. All we could see from where our car stopped was a shiny bumper. Not much else could be discerned about the car. I remembered Laura saying at the party that Richard was driving the other car to the airport.

"I could check the license plate tomorrow, Zach. You don't have to come back," I said. I was uncomfortable hanging around what looked to me like a ghost town.

"Sankar, we're here. Let's get things done instead of postponing them until the next eclipse."

Zach started walking toward the house crunching the gravel under his big feet and I felt very uneasy, as though something was crawling over me. I couldn't stop Zach from going toward the house and I didn't want to stay back and appear a total coward. So I followed him reluctantly, whispering that he should walk quietly and not make as much noise, but my voice was lost in the reverberations of his long, bold steps.

"Yep. R38 SC2 it is. And it's a red beamer," he said loudly as he stooped down. I was right behind him.

The discovery gave me no comfort for I heard Laura Blackwell's voice from behind.

"Put your hands up and turn around slowly. Don't think I won't shoot if you try anything funny."

We turned around and faced a woman with a pistol pointed at us. Like an experienced markswoman, Laura held the weapon with her right hand and braced it with her left; she was ready to shoot. Since it was so dark, I didn't expect her to recognize me. I thought of announcing myself but my mouth went dry as my heart raced.

"Would you mind telling me what you're doing in my yard?"

Given a few moments I would have come up with a plausible story. Something about a grey cat that went crawling into her front yard after being struck by our car. And about the two of us trying to find the poor beast and take it to a vet. Then compound that story with more inventions of why we were driving in that area in the first place. I am from a society that avoids confrontation at any cost, a society that does not consider temporary brushing aside of facts sinful as long as it isn't done for selfish gains and as long as it allows the parties to get cool before drawing the line. But he of the race that produced Captain

John Paul Jones, Commodore Decatur and Admiral Foregut, was the first to speak.

"Is this your car?" He asked in what I sensed as a very belligerent voice.

At that instant I saw my soul departing to that land of no return leaving a poor widow to fend for herself in a dog-eat-dog world and an orphan son selling newspapers on the street corners. The gun did not go off, though it felt like an eternity before I realized that we were still alive.

I regained my voice and said, "Laura, remember we met before. This is my friend Zach."

She gave no indication of having heard me.

"Yes, I drive it. My husband usually drives the Mercedes."

"Were you driving this car on Tuesday, last week?"

I couldn't see Laura's expression in the darkness surrounding us. She hesitated before saying, "Sankar, what's this all about?"

"You will find out soon enough," Zach said.

"It's a long story, Laura," I said in a conciliatory tone. "Perhaps we could continue some other time."

The simple fact was that I was not prepared to question Laura; I hadn't worked out a strategy and I had no idea how to proceed further with the investigation. I didn't have the authority of a police officer or the credentials of a certified private eye.

"I want to hear it now," Laura said in a stern voice. "You can't barge into my yard in the middle of the night and the walk away without explanation."

"Perhaps we could sit down somewhere," I suggested.

"We may as well go in," Laura said leading the way. She was still holding the gun, without pointing it in our direction.

"It better be good. Otherwise I'm calling the police," she said.

Chapter 17

Dropping the Ball

Z ach and I were now seated on a long sofa facing the
fireplace in Blackwell's living room. Laura sat on a heavily
cushioned chair to our left. The well-lighted room had a high
ceiling with twelve-inch wooden beams. Panels of glass formed a
wall directly right across from the entry way. Beyond that was a
balcony, perhaps projecting over a small canyon. Books and
Katchina dolls occupied the shelves on the wall behind us. It was
a beautiful place. It could have lulled me into tranquility except
for the gun within easy reach on the coffee table next to Laura.

"I want to hear the full story," Laura said.

Full story? How do I start? I decided to bring the whole
thing out in the open. There was no point in beating around the
bush this late in the game.

Instead of answering her question I said, "Laura, you
went to Gregg Westover's apartment on Tuesday last week. Am I
right?"

"Are you spying on me? God! You're spying on me."

"No, I did not. One of the students in that apartment
complex told me."

"I don't have to answer your question."

"True."

"But Sankar has to put that info in the report."

"What report?"

"The one he'll be submitting to the committee."

"That's right, Laura. I was asked to interview students who knew Gregg well and write down everything I was told."

"Really?"

"Really! Professor Fuller was clear on that."

"Jim Fuller has to have his nose in everybody's affairs. One day he is going to strep out of boundaries and then all hell breaks lose. I hope it's soon."

"But there's nothing else Sankar can do. If he doesn't put that in the report, the student might directly go to see Fuller."

I knew Zach was bluffing, but saw no reason to let Laura know. So I said, "I don't want the committee to get a wrong impression. It is perhaps better, if they know about your visit from me."

"I can tell you one thing. I was not having an affair with Gregg."

"I never suspected anything like that between you and Gregg."

"No affairs, period. With anyone. Richard and I are fully committed to keep our marriage vows."

"Good for both of you."

"Nevertheless Sankar has to mention your visit to Gregg's apartment. It would simplify matters, if we know the reason," Zach said.

"You said that before," Laura said impatiently. "Here is what happened. Gregg took something from our laboratory that doesn't belong to him. I wanted it back and I went to get it from him."

"Did you?"

"He wouldn't give it back. We had a nasty argument the second time I saw him that day."

"What is the item?"

"A lab notebook. It belongs to Richard."

"How did Gregg get hold of it?"

"I gave it to him."

"Why?"

"Gregg was Richard's student then. He wanted to browse through Richard's old notebooks. Some work Gregg was doing then depended on what Richard had done. That's what he told me. Richard keeps meticulous records. He wasn't in town and I let Gregg have a go at the records. A week or two later Gregg quit working for Richard and transferred to Frank Turner's group. Frank didn't have the decency to let us know. I didn't realize then that Gregg had swiped one of Richard's notebooks."

"When did you notice that a notebook was missing?"

"Only recently."

Those two words gave more information than Laura intended to divulge. She knew about the missing book only after Gregg started blackmailing.

"Gregg wasn't willing to return the notebook. Is that it?"

"You could've reported that to the police," Zach added.

"I didn't want to hurt a graduate student, even though he double crossed us by switching advisors without warning. I wanted Gregg to do the decent thing. I thought of going to the university police but before I could do that Gregg killed himself."

"Is there something valuable in the notebook?"

"I don't know."

"I mean valuable for Gregg."

"I just don't know."

"Why was he trying to hold on to the notebook?"

"You are asking the same question again, Sankar. I have no answer."

She was right; I was going in the same orbit. My hope was that somehow I could extract the truth from Laura by staying on the same theme. But my dear friend, Zach, had no patience. He said, rather abruptly, "He couldn't be blackmailing Richard unless he had something to go on."

"What are you talking about?"

"We know Richard faked data for two publications. We think Gregg was demanding money for his silence," Zach said.

"Nonsense! I know there are some discrepancies, but those are minor. Richard did not fake the data. He might have overlooked something. I remember when that work was done. Richard was under tremendous pressure while looking for an academic position."

"It's more serious than that. It's outright fabrication of data to suit the theory," Zach persisted.

"Stop bluffing. You don't know anything."

"I am not bluffing. Sankar told me what's in the book."

"What do you mean?"

"Sankar has the book. It is plain as paper that Richard cheated deliberately."

That turned out to be the most inappropriate statement in the whole proceedings.

I wondered, later, whether Zach would have precipitated the matter thus had he an inkling what was about to follow.

Laura suddenly grabbed the gun, jumped to where Zach was sitting and pointed it at his left temple. Looking toward me she said, "You move – all the way to the other side of the sofa." I did what I was told, frightened.

"Now I see the game you are playing. Very clever! But you are not going to get away with it."

I was too paralyzed by fear to say anything. Zach remained quiet. I couldn't see the expression on his face from where I was.

"Yes, I see your game. You got the book from Gregg and you want to take over where he left off. Is that it?"

"Gregg's stepfather gave it to me," I managed to say.

"I should have guessed. You and Gregg are in the same group. I should've guessed you were working together. Was your boss involved in this scheme too?"

"Professor Turner…

"I know he hates Richard, like all other faculty in this dump. I know they like to blow up a minor thing out of proportion to harm Richard. But you can count on it – it isn't going to happen."

"Laura, you have the wrong picture," I managed to say in spite of my dry throat.

"Shut up! Don't think I'm an idiot. I gave five grand to your sidekick and he was about to return the book. Then he found out – maybe your boss told him – that Richard's tenure papers are waiting on the provost's desk. So he upped the ante. You know all of that. Don't you?"

"Laura, you are seriously mistaken. I had no contact with Gregg. Absolutely none."

"Stop the charade. If I had some guarantee that I'd get the book back, I'd have settled for another five or ten grand. But I knew that wasn't going to work. And I can't go on throwing money to scum balls like you behind Richard's back."

"Laura, please understand. We didn't come here to…"

"I didn't want Richard to know anything about your scheme. I'll do anything to protect his reputation."

My hunch was right. Had Gregg gone directly to Richard, there would have been no tragedy. Richard would know that Gregg could not derail his career. If Gregg ever got the attention of anyone in authority, Richard could have made the whole thing look like storm in a teapot. Laura, however saw that differently. She took it too seriously; she thought, if the truth about those two papers were to come out, Richard might lose his job.

"Laura, you got it all wrong," I said, my voice recovered. I was hoping to explain things and get out of the place unharmed.

"Where is the darned notebook?"

"First I want you to hear me."

"No! I want that book now. Where is it?"

"Laura, I want to explain something.…"

"I've had enough explanation. If I don't get that notebook I am going to blow your friend's brains out. Under our laws no judge could convict me for defending my property. So, for the last time, where is the notebook?"

"In my car outside."

"Bring it in. Remember, no games, if you want your friend alive."

I did what I thought was the safest thing to do. I brought the notebook and placed it on a table next to the door, assuming we would be unceremoniously driven out of the house once Laura had her treasure. I was wrong.

Laura made Zach get up and walk toward the phone on the wall. While still pointing the gun at Zach's temple she called 911. "Two men broke into my house. I need help...."

That was when Zach screamed a loud "No." Laura was momentarily distracted and Zach violently pushed her to the floor.

"Run, you fool, run," he yelled at me while rushing out of the house. I galloped after him.

Twenty minutes later we were in Sam's sipping coffee.

"Why did you bring the notebook in?" Zach said. I got the impression he was irritated with my behavior.

"I wanted to see you alive."

"You could've distracted the witch by throwing a stone at the window. Once she's distracted I could have grabbed the gun."

There wasn't anything I could say then.

"When I said run, you could have snatched the book on your way out. Why didn't you?"

Why didn't I?

"Now you have no way of proving Laura was the killer."

Unfortunately that was true.

It was definitely past two, perhaps close to three, when we got home. Zach made himself comfortable on the sofa and I went upstairs to crawl into bed.

Chapter 18

Niles Reveals his Plan

I rushed downstairs to answer the phone. "Good morning," I said while catching my breath.

"I suppose it's technically morning yet," Niles Baxter's voice came over the phone.

It was close to eleven-thirty. Niles wanted the directions to our place. He wouldn't explain why he wanted to visit at that time.

I looked around to get myself organized. There was a note on the kitchen table from Meera:

I made *pesarattu* and stuffed it with *upma*. Zach had three before he went home. One left. Jay and I → Historical Museum.

It was a strong measure of my disorganized mind that I did not feel my mouth salivate at the mention of *pesarattu* and *upma*.

I had stayed in bed until Niles' phone call thinking about our adventure the night before. Zach was right; I botched up the whole thing. In the first place I could have said the notebook was in some safe deposit box instead of saying it was in the car. Or I could have said the notebook was already with the committee. Next, once outside, I could have distracted Laura by banging the door, stumbling to the floor or throwing something at the window. That would have given an opportunity for Zach to wrestle the gun out of her hand. Considering their relative sizes he could have done that quite easily. Lastly, I could have grabbed the damned notebook as I was rushing out of the house.

My real mistake was to undertake something without preparation. Now I had nothing to show. I couldn't tell the committee anything about the notebook or of the motive for murder without sounding like a denizen in an asylum. I could not deny having received the notebook from Cathy. Professor Czerny would definitely want to know the fate of the notebook. I was sure he heard from Cathy Quintaro about Bill Underwood's visit and the book. What would I tell the head of the depatment?

After sometime my thoughts of self-criticism diminished and I felt completely unconcerned about everything. I didn't care about Gregg or Laura – the killed and the killer. It didn't bother me that team Blackwell might have a long successful life with wealth and power in spite of the murder. I felt like an alien among the people surrounding me and drifted back into uneasy sleep.

*   *   *

"That conversation we had on Friday catalyzed my thinking," Niles said as I poured coffee into his cup. "Minutes after I left you I called Kevin Chadwick to find out about opportunities to work with him for a year. You know he is number one in my area of research and highly influential to boot. Most of us think he will get a Nobel Prize one day. He was so easy to talk to on the phone. He invited me to visit him over the weekend. Well, I flew to San Diego on the Friday midnight flight and talked to him for almost three hours on Saturday morning."

I was wondering why I was chosen to be the recipient of this information. I didn't feel any enthusiasm for Niles' plans.

"It turned out Kevin just got a huge grant with no strings attached. So he could pay me for a year, quite generously, if I want to take a study leave from this rat's nest. I am quite excited."

"Good for you," I felt obligated to say.

"I must thank you. It is that conversation we had – what two days back? Feels like years ago. It made me get off my duff and do something."

"Glad it worked out."

"Of course Philippa was upset. We had a bit of a row, to put it mildly. I don't know what's going to happen. We may go our separate ways. In the long run it may turn out to be good for both of us. You can't do anything, if all your energies are tied up in domestic problems."

"I am sorry to hear that." I wasn't. I couldn't focus my attention on what Niles was saying. I felt so remote from everyone and every activity, I just wanted to be left alone.

"Sankar, I didn't come all the way to tell you this. It could have waited until tomorrow. There is something else I want to talk to you about urgently. That's why I came directly from the airport."

Well, what is it?

"Remember what I said about Richard Blackwell at the party?"

"Vaguely."

"I said that he's the type who'd cheat on his wife. That he will dump Laura once he gets tenure."

"Yes, I remember."

"Well, Richard's frequent trips to San Diego are not for research. He is having an affair with a young first year grad student. I didn't go spying, I assure you. It's an open secret. The amorous pair doesn't conceal their cavorting."

"He's ungrateful, considering how supportive Laura had been."

"That's what I say. She gave up everything for his career. She has excellent organizational skills. Otherwise she couldn't manage his lab and accounts. She kept records for Richard's grants, corralled the graduate students into a strict schedule, took care of correspondence and many other things. She is the business manager, really. If she worked for a firm, she would have been in a position of authority by this time."

I wasn't in a mood to talk about Laura and Richard then. Otherwise I might have added my own readings on how devoted she was to Richard.

"I think she's in angel."

I was too exhausted to contradict Niles. Besides it would have taken too long to convince him to tone down his hagiolatary.

"I have a soft spot for Laura. In fact I could easily fall in love with her. I don't mind saying it to you."

What is Niles saying? Is he talking about a triangle or a quadrangle?

"I felt very strong attraction from the first time I saw her at a departmental picnic. I thought I could kill for her. But I also respect her. If she's happy with Richard, I'll accept it. I'll keep my distance."

Niles appeared moody. I got up and without asking filled his coffee cup.

He took a sip and said, "Yesterday I took Polaroid shots of Richard and his girl friend on the beach. I swear I didn't go there to spy on them. It's just they were so blatant. There was no doubt what they were up to. I could've stood right in front of them and snapped. They wouldn't have noticed."

"That was risky," I said. I didn't know whether I meant for Richard or for Niles.

"I want to show those pictures to Laura. She should know what's happening behind her back."

"That's risky," I said again without a clear idea of what I meant, but Niles paid no attention.

"I am not going to tell her my feelings. What I said is between you and me. I just want to give her the facts. That's all. She has a right to know the facts."

"I hope you are doing the right thing, Niles."

"I am going to keep my feelings locked up. I'll walk away, if she says she doesn't want to be bothered. But if Laura is depressed with the news I'll let her know what's happening is not her fault. I'll give all the sympathy she needs."

"Niles, are you sure you are doing the right thing?"

"This is not about my feelings. I want Laura to have an accurate picture of what's happening behind her back. She deserves to know."

"Be careful. It's a delicate matter."

"I know. That's why I want you to go with me."

That was a jolt.

"I can't."

"Why?" Niles wanted to know.

Niles saw an angel in Laura. I saw a monster in her, when she held Zach at gun point and threatened to shoot. Until that moment I had difficulty thinking they were one person. But now the duality disappeared. Laura was angel for Richard and monster for Gregg. What would she be for Niles who was going to show her that she was playing the angel to the wrong man?

"Any reason you don't want to go?" Niles restated.

I didn't want to describe my previous night's experience to Niles.

I said, "I feel it'd make more sense for you to see her alone. After all you are the one with pictures. Besides I work for Professor Turner. I have a feeling he isn't popular with Richard."

I saw no connection between the ideas I packed together, but that satisfied Niles. He said, "You're right. I should see her alone. Next time we can go together, if that would help."

"Yes, next time," I said just to end the conversation.

Chapter 19

A Strange Turn of Events

The following Monday was a holiday in memory of Martin Luther King, celebrated for the first time in our state. I was under the impression that the committee was going to meet nevertheless, but decided to stay home. By the time I got to the department on Tuesday the news was widespread. It was in the newspapers; it was the main item on the previous evening's TV, which I had not seen or heard. I got it first from Cathy Quintaro as I was locking my bicycle to the stand.

This was the story: Laura went to the airport on Sunday night. Among the returning passengers she saw Richard and his new girl, whose name happened to be Tami Dent. The two were so absorbed in each other they were oblivious to the rest of the world. (A woman who sat behind them in the airplane said they had behaved like newly weds.) The couple didn't see Laura until she was within arm's reach. Then Laura aimed the gun at Tami and fired two bullets; Richard jumped in front of Tami and caught both. One went into his chest and the other punctured his aorta. He died immediately. Tami ran away from the scene screaming as the guards took the gun away from Laura, who offered no resistance.

The description raised several questions in my mind. Why did Laura go to the airport? She knew Richard had his car parked there and didn't need a ride home. Why did Tami come with Richard? Did Laura know that Tami would be accompanying him? Did Niles tell Laura what he had seen? Did he show her the photographs? But I didn't want to think about these questions. I was ready to immerse myself in reading research papers and continuing with my laboratory work.

*   *   *

The first thing I noticed when I went into my lab-office was last Monday's peanut butter sandwich, showing signs of entropic disintegration. I dropped it in the trash can in the men's room and felt the act was symbolic of erasing the previous week's activities from my mind. But before I could open shop, Niles barged in.

"You weren't here yesterday."

"I stayed home."

"Remember the conversation we had on Sunday?"

"Yes, I do."

"That's between you and me. I'd appreciate if you keep it to yourself."

"I have no intention of sharing it with anyone either in the committee or outside."

"The committee is dead. Czerny officially canceled it."

"That's good news."

"You understand my precarious situation, don't you?"

"What situation?"

"I don't want to be implicated in this case. If the word ever gets around that I told Laura about Richard and Tami, I might be in trouble. You know how lawyers are. They try to put blame on everyone except the one who actually did it."

"I don't see how a lawyer could drag you into court."

"I do. You don't know about those reptiles. The simple fact is Laura shot Richard. I didn't tell her to shoot anyone. I only showed her the photos so that she could organize her life better. I was doing her a favor. That's the whole story."

Niles left after giving me a handshake.

*   *   *

"You're pardoned," Zach said when I called him later in the day and told him of Laura Blackwell's revenge on her unfaithful husband.

"For what?"

"For being a lousy detective and putting my life in danger."

His tone didn't match the criticism in those words, so I didn't see any reason to defend myself; not that I could successfully do that anyway.

"I am glad it's over," I said.

'No, it ain't"

"How is that?"

"You better write a full report on your activities and send it to the homicide guys"

"I don't see…"

"Listen, Sankar. If you don't come out in the open soon, the police could accuse you of holding back evidence. That could get you a much needed rest in county jail."

A wave of shudder went through my spine as I realized that I had to guard myself from the authorities for discovering the truth. I spent the rest of the afternoon writing a report of my involvement with Gregg's case. To be on the safe side, I claimed that I didn't suspect Laura as Gregg's killer until she pointed the gun at us, which is not far from the truth; I added that had I felt that she would go on to kill her husband, I'd have rushed to the police station to inform the detectives working on the case. I bicycled to the main police station and delivered the report personally. I was certain that Professor's Czerny and Fuller would have liked to see the report and sprinkle it with their erudite comments before forwarding it to the homicide squad, but

I didn't want to take the risk of being charged with obstruction of police investigation. I made copies of my report, however, and distributed them to Professor Czerny, my boss and the members of the now defunct committee. If they are displeased with my going over their heads, let it be so, I told myself. As it later turned out, I need not have worried about their reactions.

*   *   *

I saw Professor Fuller in the corridor a few days later while carrying a Dewar flask of liquid nitrogen back to my lab.

"I must give you credit, Sankar. You were right. We know now Gregg was murdered. You have the right intuition. A valuable gift."

I thanked him while feeling apprehensive. Compliments from a professor like Fuller often mean that he is going to draft you into doing something you would rather not.

When I checked my mailbox in the department later that day I found the following note.

Sankar,

The committee and I (personally) want to thank you for the outstanding work you have done for the Ad Hoc Committee. Keep up the good work

Czerny
Professor
Head of the Department.

Professor Susan Bond was the last one to remind me of my involvement with the committee. As I was moving toward stairs after locking my lab, I heard her voice from behind.

"Sankar, now that Richard is gone, do you know what's going to happen to that space and all that equipment he hoarded?"

"I have no idea."

"I thought you're on the committee." Before I could say that the committee had met its end, she added. "Let me know if this topic comes up for discussion. I badly need more space. And I could put the power supplies and distillation apparatus in Richard's lab to very good use."

Having said that she walked past me, giving the impression I was the one who detained her in the corridor.

I bicycled home thinking of the fish *pulusu* with tamarind sauce, mustard seeds and chilies Meera would be cooking and of a strategy to defend my chess pieces against the fierce armies of my son.

*   *   *

That spring semester, which had started with an unusual committee assignment, turned out to be one of my productive periods. My experiment worked without a hitch and the article I wrote on it was accepted in record time. A grant proposal I wrote in collaboration with Professor Turner was funded. Now I could count on staying in Gadsden for three more years even though only as an underpaid post-doc. That would give Meera a chance to finish her M.S. in computer science. Between the two of us she is the more competitive one, even though she will never admit it. I wouldn't be surprised if she were to get a more lucrative job, after finishing her master's program, while her husband continues on as a post-doc. I know that deep down she wants me to continue doing what I want to do, however critical she might sound of my obsession with research.

I wasn't offered the faculty position I craved. Indeed, no one was offered that position since the funds were given to another department that was more successful than ours in recruiting women and minorities.

*   *   *

Laura Blackwell was charged with the murder of her husband. As of now her case hasn't come to trail. I was told that the local newspapers have written extensively about her life with an abusive husband. I haven't bothered to read them, even though I feel sorry for both Richard and Laura.

*   *   *

A few days after Laura's arrest I saw Susan Bond in the mail room.

"Your committee work may be over but ours is just beginning," she said. When I told her that I had no idea what she was talking about, Susan explained. The Provost had appointed a committee to study excessive pressures on spouses of faculty members without tenure.

I didn't know then that I would soon find out the results of excessive pressure on Susan Bond's husband, Jonathan.

*   *   *

"I'm going to write an angry letter to the editor," Zach said. This was about a month after Laura was arrested.

"It's unfair. You did all the work and they get all the credit," Meera joined.

They were referring to an article in the local newspaper that described how Professors Czerny and Fuller had solved the mystery surrounding a graduate student's death. The article was accompanied by photographs of the two professors in animated discussion in the aisles of a lab. There were quotes from their statements comparing the standard method of criminal investigation with their 'diffusive committee-oriented' approach. There was also a mention of the professors' intention to offer, during the next year, an elective course that would compare detective novels with case studies of scientific discoveries, if monies were made available for such a course. Professor Czerny was quoted as saying that such a course would motivate more

American students to go into science and thus make us more competitive in the world market.

*   *   *

Toward the middle of the semester one of the minor puzzles surrounding Gregg Westover was answered. I found a letter, already opened and addressed to Gregg, in my mail box with a penciled in note from Cathy: "I thought you would like to see this." The letter informed Gregg that he was not an employee of the university as of that date. He would, however, get three months pay beyond the termination date so that he could retrain himself and reapply for another, possibly better paying, university job that ed his personality better. The letter made no sense to me, since grad students and post-docs have no way of retraining themselves other than by continuing to work in a lab and severance pay for them is unheard of. Cathy Qunitaro cleared up the mystery. To answer the public criticism that the university had become too big and too inefficient, the administration had recently brought in a personnel expert and several staff members from industry for the development of CEMS - Continuous Efficiency Monitoring System. CEMS had started firing custodial staff and grounds keepers as a way of showing that they could indeed cut down on the work force and save money. Professor Czerny's letter informing Gregg that he was fired had been directed to the CEMS office where someone, who did not know the difference between the policies that govern graduate students and grounds keepers, sent Gregg the wrong letter posthumously.

*   *   *

I was rewarded - that's how I think of it - at the end of the semester for solving the mystery of Gregg's death. It was during the last seminar of the semester. Cathy Quintaro put a note in my departmental mailbox to tell me that I was expected to attend the seminar. I was puzzled by the note since seminar attendance had always been voluntary and I had been attending without fail.

Professor Czerny addressed the audience before the speaker was introduced.

"Many of you know Gregg Westover. His promising career was cut short by a tragic turn of events. I will spare you the unnecessary details. In his memory we have established a yearly teaching award with funds generously contributed by Gregg's parents, Mr. and Mrs. William Underwood. I am very pleased to tell you that the committee chose unanimously a highly talented member of our department. Professor Fuller will introduce him to you."

Professor Fuller spoke next.

"It gives me great pleasure to announce the name of the person chosen for the Gregory Westover Teaching Award. But before I announce the name let me ask you a simple question. What is teaching? Is it lecturing? Is it scribbling on a black or white board? Is it impressing or intimidating students with one's knowledge? I believe that every one here would agree with me that true teaching is none of that. True teaching involves facilitating and encouraging learning. Once we accept that obvious premise we see that outstanding teachers are not necessarily in the classroom. They could be in the research labs, in small seminar groups, in corridors where we sometime discuss ideas or even at lunch and coffee breaks. For this year's teaching award we considered not only classroom activities but the other creative activities that should properly be called teaching. Our choice, I'm quite happy to announce, is a person with a long unpronounceable name who, fortunately for all of us, goes by the name of Sankar. Those of us who have had the opportunity to work with him know how effective a teacher he is. He is a truly inspiring teacher. I now call Dr. Sankar to come and receive this modest check as a token of our appreciation of his contribution to the improvement of teaching standards in this department."

As I received the check for a hundred dollars, my heart pounded and my knees felt weak. I looked at the audience apprehensively, afraid that somebody would get up and shout, "Imposter!" I returned to my seat in an agitated state. Professor Turner who was sitting next to me put his hand on my shoulder and said, "Don't let this go to your head. You are not the first one to get an award for teaching without teaching."

I wanted to thank him for understanding but the seminar had just started and I needed a nap badly.